Walter Crane, Mrs. Molesworth

A Christmas Child

A Sketch of a Boy-Life

Walter Crane, Mrs. Molesworth

A Christmas Child
A Sketch of a Boy-Life

ISBN/EAN: 9783337379575

Printed in Europe, USA, Canada, Australia, Japan

Cover: Foto ©Andreas Hilbeck / pixelio.de

More available books at **www.hansebooks.com**

A CHRISTMAS CHILD

A Sketch of a Boy-Life

BY

MRS. MOLESWORTH

AUTHOR OF

'CARROTS,' 'CUCKOO CLOCK,' ETC.

ILLUSTRATED BY WALTER CRANE

'O Christmas, merry Christmas!
Is it really come again?
With its memories and greetings,
With its joy and with its pain.'

London

MACMILLAN AND CO.

1880

TO

The Two Friends

WHO WILL BEST UNDERSTAND THIS

SIMPLE LITTLE STORY

I DEDICATE IT

WITH MUCH AFFECTION

PARIS, *May* 1880.

CONTENTS.

CHAPTER I.

PAGE

BABY TED 1

CHAPTER II.

IN THE GARDEN 18

CHAPTER III.

WISHES AND FEARS 37

CHAPTER IV.

THE STORY OF SUNNY 58

CHAPTER V.

THE STORY OF SUNNY (*Concluded*) . . 76

CHAPTER VI.

LITTLE NARCISSA 94

CHAPTER VII.

PAGE

GETTING BIG   116

CHAPTER VIII.

"STATISTICS"   137

CHAPTER IX.

A PEACOCK'S FEATHER AND A KISS   .   .   . 161

CHAPTER X.

SOME RAINY ADVENTURES   179

CHAPTER XI.

" IT'S ONLY I, MOTHER "   .   .   . 200

CHAPTER XII.

THE WHITE CROSS   216

LIST OF ILLUSTRATIONS.

" THE STORY OF SUNNY ".   .   .   *Frontispiece*

" I WISH THOO'D LET ME HELP THOO TO CUT THE GRASS "   .   .   .   . *To face page* 32

" SHE HUNTED ABOUT AMONG THE LEAVES AND BRANCHES TILL SHE FOUND A LITTLE SILVER KNOB " .   .   .   .   . ,, 83

" BABY SHOWED, OR TED *THOUGHT* SHE DID, A QUITE EXTRAORDINARY LOVE FOR THE BOUQUETS HER LITTLE BROTHER ARRANGED FOR HER " . ,, 98

" OH DEAR, OH DEAR ! " CRIES BEAUTY, JUMPING UP IN A FRIGHT, " HE'S COMING TO EAT ME "   . ,, 133

" THEY WERE NEATLY TACKED ON TO THE FEATHER CARD, WHICH HAD A VERY FINE EFFECT ON THE WALL OF THE MUSEUM "   .   . ,, 170

" MASTER TED, VERY WET INDEED, MADE HIS APPEARANCE WITH ROSY CHEEKS AND A GENERAL LOOK OF SELF-SATISFACTION "   . ,, 194

CHAPTER I.

BABY TED.

"Where did you get those eyes so blue?"
"Out of the sky as I came through."

CHRISTMAS WEEK a good many years ago. Not an
"old-fashioned" Christmas this year, for there was no
snow or ice; the sky was clear and the air pure, but
yet without the sharp, bracing clearness and purity
that Master Jack Frost brings when he comes to see
us in one of his nice, bright, sunny humours. For he
has humours as well as other people—not only is he
fickle in the extreme, but even *black* sometimes, and
he is then, I can assure you, a most disagreeable
visitor. But this Christmas time he had taken it into
his head not to come at all, and the world looked
rather reproachful and disconcerted. The poor, bare
December world—it misses its snow garment, so
graciously hiding all imperfections revealed by the
absence of green grass and fluttering leaves; it misses,

too, its winter jewels of icicles and hoar frost.   Poor
old world!   What a great many Decembers you have
jogged through; no wonder you begin to feel that you
need a little dressing up and adorning, like a beauty
no longer as young as she has been.   Yet ever-young
world, too!   Who, that gazes at March's daffodils
and sweet April's primroses, can believe that the
world is growing old?   Sometimes one could almost
wish that it would leave off being so exquisitely, so
heartlessly young.   For the daffodils nod their golden
heads, the primroses smile up through their leafy
nests—year after year, they never fail us.   But the
children that loved them so; the little feet that
trotted so eagerly down the lanes, the tiny hands that
gathered the flower-treasures with such delight—
where are they all?   Men and women, some in far-
off lands, perhaps; or too wearied by cares and sorrows to look for the spring flowers of long ago.   And
some—the sweetest of all, *these* seem—farther away
still, and yet surely nearer? in the happier land,
whose flowers our fancy tries in vain to picture.

But I am forgetting a little, I think, that I am
going to tell about a child to children, and that my
"tellings" begin, not in March or April, but at
Christmas-time.   Christmas-time, fortunately, does

not depend on Jack Frost for *all* its pleasures. Christmas-boxes are just as welcome without as with his presence. And never was a Christmas-box more welcome than one that came to a certain house by the sea one twenty-sixth of December, now a good many years ago.

Yet it was not a very big present, nor a very uncommon present. But it was very precious, and, to *my* thinking, very, very pretty; for it was a wee baby boy. Such a dear wee baby, I think you would have called it; so neat and tiny, and with such nice baby-blue eyes. Its hands and feet, especially, were very delightful. "*Almost* as pretty as newly-hatched ducklings, aren't they?" a little girl I know once said of some baby feet that she was admiring, and I really think she was right. No wonder was it, that the happy people in the house by the sea were very proud of their Christmas-box, that the baby's mother, especially, thought there never was, never could be, anything so sweet as her baby Ted.

But poor baby Ted had not long to wait for his share of the troubles which we are told come to all, though it does seem as if some people, and children too, had more than others. He was a very delicate little baby. His mother did not notice it at first because, you see, he was the first baby she had ever had of her very own, and she was too pleased to think him anything but perfect. And indeed he *was* perfect of his kind, only there was so little of him! He was like one of those very, very tiny little white flowers that one has to hunt under the hedges for, and which surprise you by their daintiness when you look at them closely. Only such fragile daintiness needs tender handling, and these little half-opened buds sometimes shrink from the touch of even the kindest of mothers and nurses, and gently fade out of their sight to bloom in a sunnier and softer clime than ours. And knowing this, a cold chill crept round the heart of little Ted's mother when his nurse, who was older and wiser than she, shook her head sadly as she owned that he was about the tiniest baby she had ever seen. But the cold chill did not stay there. Ted, who was scarcely a month old, gave a sudden smile of baby pleasure as she was anxiously looking at him. He had caught sight of some bright flowers on the wall, and his blue eyes had told him that the proper thing to do was to smile at them. And his smile was to his mother like the sun breaking through a cloud.

"I will not be afraid for my darling," said she.

"God knows what is best for him, but I think, I do *think*, he will live to grow a healthy, happy boy. How could a Christmas child be anything else?"

And she was right. Day after day, week by week, month after month, the wee man grew bigger and stronger. It was not all smooth sailing, however. He had to fight pretty hard for his little share of the world and of life sometimes. And many a sad fit of baby-crying made his mother's heart ache as she asked herself if after all it might not be better for her poor little boy to give up the battle which seemed so trying to him. But no—that was not Master Ted's opinion at all. He cried, and he would not go to sleep, and he cried again. But all through the crying and the restlessness he was growing stronger and bigger.

"The world strikes me as not half a bad place. I mean to look about me in it and see all that there is to be seen," I could fancy his baby mind thinking to itself, when he was held at his nursery window, and his bright eyes gazed out unweariedly at the beautiful sights to be seen from it—the mountains in the distance lifting their grand old heads to the glorious sky, which Ted looked as if he knew a good deal about if he chose to tell; the sea near at hand with its ever-changing charm and the white sails scudding along in the sunlight. Ah yes, little Ted was in the right—the world *is* a very pretty place, and a baby boy whose special corner of it is where his was, is a very lucky little person, notwithstanding the pains and grievances of babyhood.

And before lóng Ted's fits of crying became so completely a thing of the past that it was really difficult to believe in them. All his grumbling and complaining and tears were got over in these first few months. For "once he had got a start," as his nurse called it, never was there a happier little fellow. Everything came right to him, and the few clouds that now and then floated over his skies but made the sunshine seem the brighter.

And day by day the world grew prettier and pleasanter to him. It had been very pleasant to be carried out in his nurse's arms or wheeled along in his little carriage, but when it came to toddling on the nice firm sands on his own sturdy legs, and some-times—when nurse would let him—going "kite kite close" to the playful waves, and then jumping back again when they "pertended," as he said, to wet his little feet—ah, that was too delightful! And almost more delightful still was it to pick up nice smooth stones on the beach and try how far he could throw them into the sea. The sea was *so* pretty and kind, he thought. It was for a long time very difficult for him to believe that it could ever be angry and raging and wild, as he used to hear said, for of course on wet or stormy days little Ted never went down to the shore, but stayed at home in his own warm nursery.

There were pretty shells and stones and seaweed to be found on this delightful sea-shore. Ted was too little to care much for such quiet business as gathering stones and shells, but one day when he was walking with his mother she stopped so often to pick up and examine any that took her fancy, that at last Ted's curiosity was awakened.

"What is thoo doing?" he said gravely, as if not quite sure that his mother was behaving correctly, for *nurse* always told him to "walk on straight, there's a good boy, Master Ted," and it was a little puzzling to understand that mammas might do what little boys must not. It was one of the puzzles which Ted found there were a good many of in the world, and which he had to think over a good deal in his own mind before it grew clear to him. "What is thoo doing?" he asked.

"I am looking for pretty stones to take home and keep," replied his mother.

" Pitty 'tones," repeated Ted, and then he said no
more, but some new ideas had wakened in his baby
mind.

Nurse noticed that he was quieter than usual
that afternoon, for already Ted was a good deal of a
chatterbox.   But his eyes looked bright, and plainly
he had some pleasant thought in his head.   The next
day was fine, and he went off with nurse for his walk.
He looked a little anxious as they got to the turn
of the road, or rather to the joining of two roads, one
of which led to the sea, the other into country lanes.

" Thoo is doing to the sea ?" he inquired.

" Yes, dear," nurse replied, and Ted's face cleared.
When they got to the shore he trotted on quietly,
but his eyes were very busy, busier even than usual.
They looked about them in all directions, till at last
they spied what they wanted, and for half a minute
or so nurse did not notice that her little charge had
left her side and was lagging behind.

" What are you about, Master Ted ?" she said
hastily, as glancing round she saw him stooping
down—not that he had very far to stoop, poor little
man—and struggling to lift some object at his feet.

" A 'tone," he cried, "a beauty big 'tone for Ted's
muzzer," lifting in his arms a big round stone—one

of the kind that as children we used to say had dropped from the moon—which by its nice round shape and speckledness had caught his eye. "Ted will cally it hisself."

And with a very red face, he lugged it manfully along.

"Let me help you with it, dear," said nurse.

But "No, zank thoo," he replied firmly each time that the offer was repeated. "Ted must cally it his own self."

And "cally" it he did, all the way. Nurse could only succeed in getting him to put it down now and then to rest a bit, as she said, for the stone was really so big a one that she was afraid of it seriously tiring his arms. More than once she pointed out prettier and smaller stones, and tried to suggest that his mother might like them quite as well, or better; but no. The bigness, the heaviness even, was its charm; to do something that cost him an effort for mother he felt vaguely was his wish; the "lamp of sacrifice," of *self*-sacrifice, had been lighted in his baby heart, never again to be extinguished.

And, oh, the happiness in that little heart when at last he reached his mother's room, still lugging the heavy stone, and laid it at her feet!

"Ted broughtened it for thoo," he exclaimed triumphantly. And mother was *so* pleased! The stone took up its place at once on the mantelpiece as an ornament, and the wearied little man climbed up on to his mother's knee, with a look of such delight and satisfaction as is sweet to be seen on a childish face.

So Ted's education began. He was growing beyond the birds and the flowers already, though only a tiny man of three; and every day he found new things to wonder at, and admire, and ask questions about, and, unlike some small people of his age, he always listened to the answers.

After a while he found prettier presents to bring home to his mother than big stones. With the spring days the flowers came back, and Ted, who last year had been too little to notice them much, grew to like the other turning of the road almost better than that which led to the sea. For down the lanes, hiding in among the hedges, or more boldly smiling up at him in the fields, he learnt to know the old friends that all happy children love so dearly.

One day he found some flowers that seemed to him prettier than any he had ever seen, and full of delight he trudged home with a baby bouquet of them in his little hot hands. It was getting past spring into summer now, and Ted felt a little tired by the time he and his nurse had reached the house, and he ran in as usual to find his mother and relate his adventures.

" Ted has broughtened some most beauty flowers," he eagerly cried, and his mother stooped down to kiss and thank him, even though she was busy talking to some ladies who had come to see her, and whom Ted in his hurry had hardly noticed. He glanced round at them now with curiosity and interest. He rather liked ladies to come to see his mother, only he would have liked it still better if they would have just let him stay quietly beside her, looking at them and listening to what they said, without noticing him. But that way of behaving would not have seemed kind, and as Ted grew older he understood this, and learnt that it was right to feel pleased at being spoken to and even kissed.

" How well Ted is looking," said one of the ladies to his mother. " He is growing quite a big, strong boy. And what pretty flowers he has brought you. Are you very fond of flowers, my little man ?"

" Ses," said Ted, looking up in the lady's face.

" The wild flowers about here are very pretty," said another of the ladies.

" Very pretty," said his mother; " but it is curious, is it not, that there are no cowslips in this country? They are such favourites of mine. I have such pleasant remembrances of them as a child."

She turned, for Ted was tugging gently at her sleeve. " What is towslips?" he asked.

" Pretty little yellow flowers, something like primroses," said his mother.

" Oh!" said Ted. Then nurse knocked at the door, and told him his tea was ready, and so he trotted off.

" Mother loves towslips," he said to himself two or three times over, till his nurse asked him what he was talking about.

" But there's no cowslips here," said nurse, when he had repeated it.

" No," said Ted; " but p'raps Ted could find some. Ted will go and look to-morrow with nursey."

" To-morrow's Sunday, Master Ted," said nurse; " I'll be going to church."

" What's church?" he asked.

" Church is everybody praying to God, all together in a big house. Don't you remember, Master Ted?"

" Oh ses, Ted 'members," he replied. " What's praying to 'Dod, nurse?"

"Why, I am sure you know that, Master Ted. You must have forgotten. Ask your mamma again."

Ted took her advice. Later in the evening he went downstairs to say good-night. His mother was outside, walking about the garden, for it was a beautiful summer evening. Ted ran to her; but on his way something caught his eye, which sent a pang to his little heart. It was the bunch of flowers he had gathered for her, lying withered already, poor little things, on a bench just by the door, where she had laid them when saying good-bye to her visitors. Ted stopped short; his face grew very red, and big tears rose slowly to his eyes. He was carefully collecting them together in his little hand when his mother called to him.

"Come, Ted, dear," she said; "what are you about?"

More slowly than his wont Ted trotted towards her. "Muzzer doesn't care for zem," he said, holding out his neglected offering. "Poor f'owers dies when they's leaved out of water."

"My darling," said his mother with real sorrow in her voice, "I am so sorry, so very sorry, dear little Ted," and she stooped to kiss him. "Give them to me now, and I will *always* keep them."

Ted was quickly consoled.

"Zem's not towslips," he said regretfully. "Ted would like towslips for muzzer." And then with a quick change of thought he went on, "What is praying to 'Dod?" he said, looking up eagerly with his bright blue eyes.

"Praying to God means asking Him anything we want, and then He answers us. Just as you ask me something, and I answer you. And if what we ask is good for us, He gives it us. That is one way of answering our prayers, but there are many ways. You will understand better when you are bigger, dear little Ted."

Ted asked no more, but a bright pleased look came into his face. He was fond of asking questions, but he did not ask silly ones, nor tease and tease as some children do, and, as I said, when he got an answer he thought it well over in his little head till he got to understand, or thought he understood. Till now his mother had thought him too little to teach him to say his prayers, but now in her own mind she began to feel he was getting old enough to say some simple prayer night and morning, and she resolved to teach him some day soon.

So now she kissed him and bade him good-night.

"God bless my little boy," she said, as she patted his head with its soft fair hair which hung in pretty careless curls, and was cut across the forehead in front like one of Sir Joshua Reynolds' cherubs. "God bless my little boy," she said, and Ted trotted off again, still with the bright look on his face.

He let nurse put him to bed very "goodly," though bed-time never came very welcomely to the active little man.

"Now go to sleep, Master Ted, dear," said nurse as she covered him up and then left the room, as she was busy about some work that evening.

Ted's room was next to his mother's. Indeed, if the doors were left open, it was quite easy to talk one to the other. This evening his mother happened to go upstairs not long after he had been tucked into bed. She was arranging some things in her own room, moving about quietly not to waken him, if, as she hoped, he had fallen asleep, for falling asleep did not come so easily to Ted as to some children. He was too busy in his mind, he had too many things to think about and wonder about for his brain to settle itself quietly all in a minute. And if he had a strong wish, I think it was that going-to-bed time should never come at all!

For a minute or two no sound reached Ted's mother.

"I do hope he is asleep," she said to herself, but just then she stopped short to listen. Ted was speaking to himself softly, but clearly and distinctly. What could he be saying? His mother listened with a smile on her face, but the smile grew into a sort of sweet gravity as she distinguished the words. Little Ted was *praying*. He had not waited for her to teach him—his baby-spirit had found out the simple way for itself—he was just asking God for what he wanted.

"Please, dear 'Dod," he said, "tell me why thoo won't make towslips grow in this countly. Muzzer loves zem so."

Then came a perfect silence. Ted seemed to be holding his breath in expectation, and somehow his mother too stood as still as could be. And after a minute or two the little voice began again.

"Please, dear 'Dod, *please* do tell me," and then the silence returned as before. It did not last so long, however, this time—not more than a minute at most had passed when a sound of faint crying broke upon Ted's mother's hearing—the little fellow had burst into tears.

Then his mother could stay away no longer.

"What is the matter, my boy?" she said; anxious, baby though he was, not to make him feel ashamed of his innocent prayers by finding that she had overheard what he had said when he thought himself alone.

"What is my Ted crying about?"

The tears, which had stopped for an instant, came back again.

"Muzzer," he said, "'Dod *won't* 'peak to Ted. Ted p'ayed and p'ayed, and Ted was kite kite kiet, but 'Dod didn't 'amswer.' Is 'Dod a'leep, muzzer?"

"No, my boy, but what was it that Ted wanted so much?"

"Ted wanted towslips for muzzer, but 'Dod *won't* amswer," he repeated piteously.

A shower of kisses was mother's answer, and gently and patiently she tried to make him understand the *seeming* silence which had caused his innocent tears. And, as was Ted's "way," he listened and believed. But "some day," he said to his mother, "some day," would she not take him to "a countly where towslips *did* grow?"

C

CHAPTER II.

IN THE GARDEN.

"Heigh ho! daisies and buttercups,
Sweet wagging cowslips, they bend and they bow."
SONGS OF SEVEN.

DOWN below the garden of Ted's pretty home flowed, or danced rather, with a constant merry babble, a tiny stream. A busy, fussy stream it was, on its way to the beautiful little river that, in its turn, came rushing down through a mountain-gorge to the sea. I must tell you about this mountain-gorge some time, or, if you like, we shall visit it with Ted and his faithful companion, whom you have not yet heard about—his father's great big Scotch collie dog, Cheviott.

You don't know what a dear dog he was, so brave, but so gentle and considerate. He came of a brave and patient race, for you know "collies" are the famous Scotch sheep-dogs, who to their shepherd masters are more useful than any *two*-legged servant could be. And though I am not sure that "Chevie" himself had ever had to do with "the keeping of sheep," like gentle Abel of old, yet, no doubt, as a baby doggie in his northern home, he must have heard a good deal about it—no doubt, if his tongue had had the power of speaking, he could have told his little master some strange stories of adventures and narrow escapes which had happened to members of his family. For up in the Border mountains where he was born, the storms sometimes come on so suddenly that shepherd and flock are all but lost, and but for their faithful collies, might never find their way home again. Often, too, in the early spring-time, the poor little lambs go astray, or meet with some accident, such as being caught in the bushes and being unable to escape. What, then, would become of them but for their four-footed guardian, who summons aid before it is too late, and guides the gentle, silly lambkins and their mothers along the right paths? I think Ted's father and mother did well when they chose for their boy a collie like Cheviott for his companion.

Across the stream, just at the foot of the garden path which sloped down from the house, a couple of planks were placed as a bridge. A narrow bridge, and not a very firm one, it must be confessed, and perhaps for that very reason—because there was something a little risky and dangerous about it—Ted, true boy that he was, was particularly fond of crossing it. He liked to stand on it for a minute or two on the way, "jigging" up and down to feel the shaking and trembling of the planks, but that, of course, was only a kind of playing with danger. I don't think he *would* have much liked a sudden tumble into the mischievous little brook's cold waters, very cold it would have felt, though it looked so browny bright and tempting. And many a bath in the brook Ted would have had, had Chevie been as much carried away by his spirits as his little master. For no sooner did the two set off running from the top of the sloping garden path, than Ted would call out, " A race, Chevie, a race ! Who'll be at the bridge first ?" And on he would run as fast as his sturdy wee legs could carry him, Cheviott bounding beside him with a great show of also doing *his* best. But—and wasn't this clever of Chevie ?—just a little way on this side of the bridge he would—not stop short, for that might have disappointed Ted and made him feel as if they weren't having a *real* race, but go gradually more slowly, as if he felt he had no chance of gaining, so that little Ted always reached the bridge first, and stood shouting with glee and triumph. The first time or two that Ted's mother saw this little performance she had been frightened, for if the dog had gone on at full speed, or even only at luggage-train speed, beside the boy, he could not have avoided tumbling him into the brook. But for anything of this kind Cheviott was far too much of a gentleman, and after watching them once or twice, Ted's mother felt perfectly satisfied that the little man could not be better taken care of than by his four-footed friend.

There was another friend, too, who could very well be trusted to take care of Ted, for though he had, of course, a very kind, good nurse in the house, nurses are not able to be the whole day long in the garden, nor are they always very fond of being much there. So, even though Ted was still quite a little boy, it was very nice for him to have two such good out-door friends as Cheviott and David the gardener, the other one I am going to tell you of.

It was a beautiful spring day. Ted woke up early, and thought to himself how nice and bright and sunny it was going to be in the garden. He was rather in a hurry to be dressed, for there were several things he was in a hurry to do, and the days, in summer time especially, never seemed long enough for all he had before him. Just now these summer days seemed really brimming over with nice things, for his big cousin Percy—at least he was what *Ted* counted a "big" cousin, and he was a good many years older than Ted—was with him for the holidays, and though Percy had some lessons to do, still they had a good deal of time together.

"Ted wonders if Percy is 'decked' yet," said Ted to his nurse. "Decked" was the word he always used for "dressed," and he was often made fun of for using it. His mind was very full of Percy this morning, for he had only arrived the evening before, and besides the pleasure of having him with him, which was *always* a pleasure, there was the nice newness of it,—the things he had to show Percy, the tricks Chevie had learnt, big dog though he was, the letters and little words Ted had himself mastered since Percy was last there.

"I don't know that Master Percy will be ready quite so early this morning," said nurse. "He may be a little tired with travelling yesterday."

"Ted doesn't *zink* Percy will be tired," said Ted. "Percy wants to see the garden. Percy is *so* big, isn't he, nurse? Percy can throw sticks up in the

sky *so* high. Percy throwed one up in the sky up to
heaven, so high that it *never* comed down again."

"Indeed," said nurse; "are you quite sure of that,
Master Ted? Perhaps it did come down again, but
you didn't see it."

Nurse was a sensible person, you see. She did
not all at once begin saying to Ted that he was talking nonsense, or worse still that he was telling stories.
For very little children often "romance" in a sweet
innocent way which has nothing whatever to do with
story-telling—I mean *untruth*-telling, for it is better
not to call untruths "stories," is it not? The world
and the people in it, and the things they see and hear,
are all new and strange to the little creatures so lately
started on their puzzling journey. What wonder
that real and fancy are mixed up together sometimes
—that it is difficult to understand that the pretty
blue-bells do not sometimes tinkle in the moonlight,
or that there are no longer bears in the woods or
fairies hidden among the grass? Perhaps it would
be better for us if we were *more* ready to believe even
such passed-by fancies, than to be so quick as we
sometimes are to accuse others of wishing to deceive.

Ted looked at nurse thoughtfully.

"P'raps it did," he said. "P'raps it might have
comed down again after Ted was a'leep."

"I daresay it caught in a tree or something of that kind," said nurse, as she finished brushing Ted's soft curls and lifted him off the chair on which he had been standing, just as Percy put his head in at the door to ask if Ted might have a run in the garden with him before breakfast.

"They're not down yet," said Percy, nodding his bright curly head in the direction of Ted's father's and mother's room; "they're not ready. Nurse, do let Ted come out with me for a bit before breakfast," and Ted trotted off, his hand in Percy's, in utmost content.

Was there ever so clever and kind and wonderful a big boy as Percy before? Was there ever one who knew so much about *everything*—cricket and croquet and football; skating and fishing and climbing trees—things on earth and things in water—what was there he didn't know? These were the thoughts that were busy in Ted's little brain as he followed kind Percy about the garden, that bright summer morning, chattering incessantly, and yet ready enough to be silent when Percy took it into his head to relate to his tiny adorer some of his school experiences.

"Ted will go to school some day, Percy," he said half questioningly.

"Of course you will. I hope you'll come to my

school if I've not left by then. I could look after you, you know, and see that they didn't bully you."

"What's 'bully'?" asked Ted.

"Oh, teasing, you know. Setting you down because you're a little chap, and all that. Knocking you about if you don't look sharp. All those kinds of things that big fellows do to small ones."

Ted opened his eyes. It was not very clear to him what Percy meant—it was a new idea, and would have distressed him greatly had he quite taken it in that big boys could be anything but good to little ones.

"Thoo doesn't knock Ted about, and thoo is big, Percy," he said, remonstratingly.

"No, of course I don't, but that's different. You're like my brother, you know."

"And bruvvers *couldn't* knock theirselves about," said Ted with an air of satisfaction.

"N-no, I suppose not," said Percy. Boy as he was, he felt somehow that he could not bear to destroy little Ted's beautiful faith. "But never mind about that just now," he added; "let's run down the bank and see how the cabbages and cauliflowers are getting on. They were just put in when I was here last;" and for some time both boys were intensely interested in examining the state of the vegetable beds.

"Ted likes f'owers best," said the child, after a few moments' silence. "When Ted——"

"Why don't you say 'I' and 'I like,' Teddy?" said Percy. "You're getting such a big boy—four years old."

"Ted *means* I," persisted the small man. "*I* sall have all f'owers in Ted's garden, when me is big."

Percy was obliged to leave off what he was about —hunting for the slugs and caterpillars among the cabbages—in order that he might stand still and laugh.

"I'm afraid you wouldn't get the prize for grammar at our school, Ted," he said. But Ted only laughed too.

"I haven't learnt grammar," he said slowly and distinctly. "But please, Percy, Ted doesn't like cabbages. Come and see the f'owers. There was lots of c'ocodiles at that side. Ted likes zem best of all, but zem's done now."

"*Crocodiles*," said Percy. "What can crocodiles be?"

"Little f'owers with pointy leaves," said Ted. "P'raps it isn't c'ocodiles but somesing like coc— coco——"

"Crocuses perhaps," said Percy, as they made their way up to the house. "Yes, they're very pretty, but they're soon done."

" When I'm big I'll have a garden where they'll *never* be done," said Ted. " I'll have c'ocodiles and towslips for muzzer and—and——"

" Come in to breakfast, my man," called out his father from the dining-room. " What have you been about this morning ?"

"We'se been in the garden," said Ted, "and Percy's been 'samining the cabbages. He's caught slugs upon slugs, worms upon worms, earwigs upon earwigs."

" My dear little boy," said Ted's father, though he couldn't help laughing, " you mustn't learn to exaggerate."

What's 'saggerate ?" began Ted, but looking round another idea caught him. " Where's muzzer ?" he said suddenly.

" Mother is rather tired this morning," said his father. " Eat your breakfast, dear," and then he turned to talk to Percy and ask him questions as to how he was getting on at school.

For a minute or two neither of them noticed Ted. He sat quietly at his place, his bowl of bread and milk before him, but he made no attempt to eat it. Then Percy happened to see him.

" Aren't you hungry, Ted ?" he said.

Ted looked up with his two blue eyes full of tears.

"Ses," he said, "Ted's hungry. But if muzzer doesn't come down Ted can't eat. Ted won't eat nothing all day, and he'll die."

"Not quite so bad as that," said his father quietly, for he did not want Ted to see that it was difficult not to smile at his funny way of speaking, "for see here is mother coming."

Ted danced off his seat with pleasure.

"It's dedful when thoo's not here," he said feelingly, and now the bread and milk was quickly despatched. "When I'm big," he continued, in the intervals of the spoonfuls, "I'll have a house as big— as big as a mountain," his eyes glancing out of the window, "and all the little boys in the world shall live there with all their favers and muzzers, and Percies, and everybodies, and nobody shall never go away, not to school or bidness, or nothing, so that they'll all be togever always."

Ted looked round for approval, and then took another spoonful.

"What a nice place you'll make of the world, my boy, when you're big," said his father.

"Ses," said Ted with satisfaction.

"But as that time hasn't come yet, I'm afraid I *must* go to my 'bidness,'" his father went on. For he had to go several times a week a good way into the country, to see that his men were all doing their work properly. "And Percy must go with me to-day," he went on, "for he needs some new clothes, and I shall be driving through A——," which was the nearest town to which they lived.

Percy's face looked very pleased, but Ted's grew rather sad.

"Never mind, Teddy," whispered Percy. "We'll have lots of days. You must have a good game with Chevie to keep up your spirits."

"And David is going to cut the grass to-day," said his father, "so you will have plenty of fun."

"But Ted must be careful," said his mother; "don't touch David's sharp tools, Ted. I was quite frightened the other day," she added; "Ted was trying to open and shut those great big shears for clipping the borders."

"Zem was sticked fast," said Ted. "Zem opens kite easy sometimes."

"Well, don't you touch them any way," said his mother, laughing. But though Ted said "No," I don't feel sure that he really heard what his mother was saying. His wits were already off, I don't know where to—running after Cheviott perhaps, or farther

away still, up among the little clouds that were
scudding across the blue sky that he caught sight of
out of the window.

And then his father and Percy set off, and his
mother went away about her housekeeping, sending
Ted up to the nursery, and telling him that he might
ask nurse to put his big blouse on, so that he might play
about the garden without risk of soiling his clothes.

Ted felt, for him, a very little sad as he trotted
out into the garden. He had hoped for such a nice
merry day with Percy. But low spirits never
troubled him long. Off he set with Cheviott for the
race down to the little bridge, always the first bit of
Ted's programme, and careful Chevie as usual pulled
up in plenty of time to avoid any risk of toppling
his master into the brook. Arrived on the bridge,
Ted stood still and "jigged" a little as usual. Then
he peered down at the shiny water with the bright
brown pebbles sparkling up through it, and wondered
what it would feel like to be a little fish.

"Little fisses," he said to himself, "always has
each other to play with. They don't go to school,
and they hasn't no bidness, nor no cooks that they
must be such a long time ordering the dinners with,
nor—nor beds to make and stockings to mend. , I

wish nurse would 'tum out this morning. Ted doesn't like being all alone. Ted would like somebody littler to play with, 'cos then they wouldn't go to school or out d'ives with papa."

But just as he was thinking this, he caught sight of some one coming across the garden, and his ideas took another turn at once.

"David, old David," he cried, "is thoo going to cut the grass? Do let me come and help thoo, David."

And he ran back across the bridge again and made his way to David as fast as he could.

"Good morning, Master Ted," said the gardener. "Is it beautiful day, Master Ted, to be sure. Yes indeed."

"Ses," agreed Ted. "Good morning, old David. I'm going to stay out in the garden a long time, a tevible long time, 'cos it's such a sprendid lovely day. What is thoo going to do, David? Can't Ted help thoo?"

"I am going to cut the grass, Master Ted, but I not be very long—no; for it is only the middle that's be cut. All the rest stand for hay, to be sure. Ay, indeed."

"And when will the hay be cuttened?" inquired Ted.

"That's be as Master order, and not as Master can choose neither—no," said David. "He not able to make for the sun to shine; no, indeed; nor the rain neither,—no."

"*'Dod* sends rain and sun," said Ted, reverently, but yet looking at David with a sort of curiosity.

"Well, indeed you are right, Master Ted. Yes, yes. But I must get on with my work. God gives us work to do, too; ay, indeed; and them as not work never expect to eat, no, never; they not care for their victual anyhow if they not work for it. No."

Ted looked rather puzzled. "Ted eats," he said, —"not victuals—Ted doesn't know that meat—but bread and butter, and tea, and potatoes, and rice pudding, and meat, and *sometimes* 'tawberry jam and apple pie and—and—lots of things. And Ted likes zem very much, but him doesn't work."

"I not know for that, Master Ted," said David, "is it all kinds of work; ay, indeed; and I see you very near always busy—dear me, yes; working very good, Master Ted—ay."

"I *like* to be busy. I wish thoo'd let me help thoo to cut the grass," said Ted, eyeing David wistfully, as he started his big scythe, for the old gardener knew nothing of mowing machines, and would most

" I wish thoo'd let me help thoo to cut the grass."—P. 32.

likely have looked upon them with great contempt. But he stopped short a moment to look down at wee Ted, staring up at him and wishing to be in his place.

"No, indeed, Master Ted *bach !*" he said; "you soon have your cliver little legs and arms cut to pieces, if you use with my scythe, Master Ted—ay, indeed, d'rectly. It look easy, to be sure, but it not so easy even for a cliver man like you, Master Ted—no, indeed. But I tell you what you shall do. You shall help to make the grass to a heaps, and then I put it in a barrow and wheel it off. Ay, indeed; that be the best."

This proposal was very much to Ted's taste. Chevie and he, at a safe distance from David's scythe, thought it great fun to toss about the soft fine grass and imagine they were helping David tremendously. And after a while, when Chevie began to think he had had enough of it, and with a sort of condescending growl by way of explanation, stretched himself out in the sunshine for a little forenoon sleep, David left off cutting, and, with Ted's help of course, filled the barrow and wheeled it off to the corner where the grass was to lie to be out of the way. It was beginning to be rather hot, though still quite early, and Ted's face grew somewhat red with his exertions as he ran beside David.

D

" You better ride now ; jump in, Master Ted," said the gardener, when his barrow was empty. So he lifted him in and wheeled him back to the lawn, which was *quite* after Ted's own heart.

" Isn't thoo going to cut with thoo's big scissors?" said Ted after a while.

" It is want oiling," said David, " and I forget to do them. I shall leave the borders till after dinner, —ay, sure," and he was going on with his scything when suddenly a voice was heard from the house calling him.

" David, David, you're wanted," said the voice, and then the cook made her appearance at the side of the house. " There's a note to take to ——."

They could not hear to where, but David had to go. He glanced round him, and, afraid of Ted's experiments, shouldered his scythe and walked off with it for fear of accidents.

" Are you going in, Master Ted ? " he asked.

" Nurse is going to call me when she's ready," said Ted composedly, and knowing that the little fellow often played about by himself for a while, good David left him without any more anxiety. He had got his scythe safe, he never thought of the big pair of shears he had left lying in the grass !

Now these gigantic "scissors" as he called them had always had a wonderful attraction for Ted. He used to think how funny they would look beside the very tiny fine pair his mother worked with—the pretty scissors that lay in her little case lined with velvet and satin. Ted had not, in those days, heard of Gulliver and his strange adventures, but if he had, one might have imagined that to his fancy the two pairs of scissors were like a Brobdignag and a Lilliputian. And no sooner had David disappeared than unfortunately the great scissors caught his eyes.

"Zem's still sticked fast," he said to himself. "David says zem needs oil. Wiss I had some oil. P'raps the fissy oil to make Ted grow big would do. But the scissors is big enough. Ted wonders if the fissy oil would make zem bigger. Zem *couldn't* be much bigger."

Ted laughed a little to himself at the funny fancy. Then he sat and stared at the scissors. What did they remind him of? Ah yes, they were like the shears of "the great, long, red-legged scissor man," in the wonderful story of "Conrad Suck-a-thumb," in his German picture-book. Almost, as he gazed at them, it seemed to Ted that the figure of the scissors

man would suddenly dart out from among the bushes
and seize his property.

"But him wouldn't cut *Ted's* fumbs," thought the
little man to himself, "'cos Ted *never* sucks zem.
What a pity the scissors is sticked fast! Poor David
can't cut with zem. P'raps Ted could oilen zem for
poor David! Ted will go and get some fissy oil."

No sooner thought than done. Up jumped Ted,
and was starting off to the house when a growl from
Cheviott made him stop. The dog had just awakened,
and seeing his little master setting off somewhere
thought it his business to inquire where to and why.
He lifted his head and gave it a sort of sleepy shake,
then growled again, but gently of course.

"What did thoo say, Chevie?" said Ted. "Did
thoo want to know where I was going? Stay here,
Chevie. Ted will be back in a minute—him's on'y going to get some fissy oil to oilen poor David's scissors."

And off he set, though a third growl from Cheviott
followed him as he ran.

"What does Chevie mean?" thought Ted. "P'raps
him's thinking muzzer said Ted mustn't touch zem
big scissors. But muzzer on'y meant Ted wasn't to
cutten with zem. Muzzer would *like* Ted to help
poor David," and, his conscience quite at rest, he
trotted on contentedly.

CHAPTER III.

WISHES AND FEARS.

Children. " Here are the nails, and may we help?
    Jessie. You shall if I should want help.
Children. Will you want it then?
      Please want it—we like helping."

THERE was no one in the nursery, fortunately for
Ted's plans. *Un*fortunately rather, we should perhaps say, for if nurse had been there, she would have
asked for what he wanted the little bottle which had
held the cod-liver oil, that he had lately left off
taking, but of which a few drops still remained.

Ted climbed on to a chair and reached the shelf
where it stood, and in two minutes he was off again,
bottle in hand, in triumph. He found Cheviott lying
still, where he had left him; he looked up and
yawned as Ted appeared, and then growled with an
air of satisfaction. It was sometimes a little difficult
for Chevie to decide exactly how *much* care he was
to take of Ted. After all, a little two-legged boy

that could talk was not *quite* the same as a lamb, or even a sheep. He could not run round him barking, to prevent his trotting where he wished—there were plainly some things Ted had to do with and understood which Chevie's dog-experience did not reach to.

So Cheviott lay there and blinked his honest eyes in the sunshine, and stared at Ted and wondered what he was after now! For Ted was in a very tip-top state of delight! He sat down cross-legged on the grass, drew the delicious big shears to him— they were heavy for him even to pull—and uncorking the bottle of " fissy" oil, began operations.

" Zem *is* sticked fast, to be soore," he said to himself, adopting David's favourite expression, as he tugged and tugged in vain. " If thoo could hold one side and Ted the other, they would soon come loosened," he observed to Cheviott. But Cheviott only growled faintly and blinked at his master sleepily, and after a good deal more tugging Ted did manage to open the shears, which indeed at last flew apart so sharply that the boy toppled over with the shock, and rolled for a moment or two on the grass, though happily not on the shears, before he recovered his balance.

Laughing merrily, he pulled himself up again. Luckily the bottle had not been overturned. Ted poured a drop or two carefully on to his fingers, quite regardless of the fishy smell, and proceeded to anoint the scissors. This he repeated several times, polishing them all over till they shone, but not understanding that *the* place where the oil was needed was the hinge, he directed the best of his attention to the general shininess.

Then he sat and looked at them admiringly.

" *Won't* David be p'eased?" he said. " Zem's oilened all over now. Ted must see if they don't sticken fast now."

With nearly as much difficulty as he had had to open them, Ted now managed to shut them.

" Zem's better," thought the busy little man, " but Ted must see how they cut."

He laid them flat on the grass, at a place where the blades had not been completely sheared by the scythe. Tug number one—the oil had really done some good, they opened more easily—tug number two, behold them gaping—tug number three, they bite the grass, and Ted is just going to shout in triumph when a quick shock of pain stabs through him. He had been kneeling almost *on* the shears, and their cruel jaws had snipped, with the grass, the tender fleshy part of his poor little leg!

It was not the pain that frightened him so much as the feeling held fast by the now dreadful scissors.

"David, David," he cried, "oh, please come. Nurse, please come. Ted has cuttened hisself."

His little voice sounded clear and shrill in the summer quiet of the peaceful garden, and nurse, who had been hastening to come out to him, heard it from the open window. David too was on his way back, and poor Ted was soon released. But it was a bad cut—he had to be carried into the house to have it bathed and sponged and tenderly bound up by mother's fingers. He left off crying when he saw how sorry mother looked.

"Ted is *so* sorry to t'ouble thoo," he said.

"And mother is sorry for Ted," she replied. "But, my dear little boy," she went on, when the poor leg was comfortable and its owner forgetting its pain on mother's knee, "don't you remember that mother told you not to touch David's tools?"

"Oh ses," he replied. "Ted wouldn't touch zem for hisself, but it was to *help David*," and the innocent confidence with which he looked up in her face went to his mother's heart.

"But *still*, dear Ted, you must try to understand that what mother says, you must do exactly. Mother

likes you to be kind and helping to people, but still
mother knows better than you, and that is why, when
she tells you things, you must remember to do what
she says."

Ted looked grave and a little puzzled, and seeing
this his mother thought it best to say no more just
then. The lesson of obedience was one that Ted
found rather puzzling, you see, but what his mother
had said had made a mark in his mind. He thought
about it often, and as he grew bigger other things
happened, as you will hear, to make him think of it
still more.

It was rather a trial to Ted not to be able to run
about as usual that afternoon, for had he done so, the
cut might have begun to bleed again, so he had to sit
still in the nursery, looking out at the window and
hoping and hoping that Percy would soon come back.
Once David and his barrow passed underneath, and
the gardener called up to know if Master Ted's leg
was better. Ted shook his head rather dolefully.

" Him's better," he said, " but Ted can't run about.
Ted's so sad, David. Muzzer's got letters to write and
Percy's out."

A kind thought struck David. He went round to
the drawing-room window and tapped at it gently.

Ted's mother was writing there. Might he wheel Master Ted in his barrow to the part of the garden where he was working?—he would take good care of him—"the little gentleman never cut himself if I with him—no, indeed; I make him safe enough."

And Ted's mother consented gladly. So in a few minutes he was comfortably installed on a nice heap of dry grass, with Cheviott close beside him and David near at hand.

"You never touch my tools again, Master Ted, for a bit; no, to be sure; do you now?" said David.

"No," said Ted. "Muzzer says I mustn't. But wasn't the big scissors nicely oilened, David?"

"Oh, fust rate—ay," said David. "Though I not say it is a cliver smell—no. I not like the smell, Master Ted."

"Never mind," replied Ted reassuringly. "Ted will ask muzzer for some cock-alone for thoo. Thoo can put some on the scissors."

"What's that, Master Ted?" inquired David, who was not at all above getting information out of his little master.

"Cock-alone," repeated Ted. "Oh, it's somesing that smells very nice. I don't know what it is. I thing it must be skeesed out of f'owers. I'll run and get thoo some now, David, this minute," and he was on the point of clambering to his feet when the stiff feeling of his bandaged leg stopped him. "Oh, I forgot," he exclaimed regretfully.

"Yes indeed, Master Ted. You not walk a great deal to-day, to be sure—no, indeed—for a bit; ay."

Ted lay still for a minute or two. He was gazing up at the sky, which that afternoon was very pure and beautiful.

"Who paints the sky, David?" he said suddenly.

"Well indeed, Master Ted, I not think you ask me such a foolis' question, Master Ted *bach !*" said David. "Who's make a sky and a sea and everything so?"

"'Dod," said Ted. "Oh, I know that. But I thoughtened p'raps 'Dod put somebody up there to paint it. It was *so* pitty last night, David—*all* tolours —Ted tan't say zem all. Why isn't there many tolours now, David?"

"I not know for sure," said David, stopping a moment in his work and looking up at the sky.

"Ted *thought*," continued the little fellow slowly, "Ted *thought* p'raps 'Dod's paints was getting done. Could that be why?"

David was rather matter-of-fact, and I don't know

that that made him any the worse a companion for Ted, whose brain was already quite full enough of fancies. So he did not smile at Ted's idea, but answered quite gravely,

"No indeed, Master Ted, I not think that untall."

"If on'y Ted could fly," the child continued in a minute or two, as just then a flock of birds made their graceful way between his gazing eyes and the clear blue vault above. "How pittily birds flies, don't they, David? If Ted could fly he'd soon find out all about the sky and everysing. And it wouldn't matter then that him had hurt his leg. *Couldn't* Ted learn to fly, David?"

Ted was soaring too far above poor David's head already for him to know what to answer. What could he say but "No indeed, Master Ted," again? He had never heard tell of any one that could fly except the angels. For David was fond of going to church, or chapel rather, and though he could not read Ted's Bible, he could read his own very well.

"Angels," said Ted. The word started his busy fancy off in a fresh direction. He lay looking up still, watching now the lovely little feathery clouds that began to rise as the sun declined, and fancying they were angels with wings softly floating hither and thither in the balmy air. He watched one little group, which seemed to him like three angels with their arms twined together, so long, that at last his eyes grew rather tired of watching and their little white blinds closed over them softly. Little Ted had fallen asleep.

"So, so; dear me, he tired," said old David, as, surprised at the unusual silence, he turned to see what Ted was about. "Bless him, he tired very bad with his cliver talk and the pain; ay—but, indeed, he not one to make fuss—no. He a brave little gentleman, Master Ted—ay, indeed," and the kind old man lifted the boy's head so that he should lie more comfortably, and turned his wheelbarrow up on one side to shade him from the sun.

Ted smiled in his sleep as David looked at him. Shall I tell you what made him smile? In his sleep he had got his wish. He dreamt that he was flying. This was the dream that came to him.

He fancied he was running down the garden path with Chevie, when all at once Chevie seemed to disappear, and where he had been there stood a pretty snow-white lamb. With an eager cry Ted darted forward to catch it, and laid his hand on its soft woolly coat, when—it was no lamb but a little cloud he was trying to grasp. And wonderful to say, the little cloud seemed to float towards him and settle itself on his shoulders, and then all of himself Ted seemed to find out that it had turned into wings!

"Ted can fly, Ted can fly!" he cried with delight, or *thought* he cried. In reality it was just then that David lifted his head, and feeling himself moving, Ted fancied it was the wings lifting him upward, and gave the pleased smile which David noticed. Fly! I should think so. He mounted and mounted, higher and higher, the white wings waving him upwards in the most wonderful way, till at last he found himself right up in the blue sky where he had so wished to be. And ever so many—lots and lots of other little white things were floating or flying about, and, looking closely at them, Ted saw that they were not little clouds as they seemed at first, but wings—all pairs of beautiful white wings, and dear little faces were peeping out from between them. They were all little children like himself.

"Come and play, Ted, come and play. Ted, *Ted*, TED!" they cried so loud, that Ted opened his eyes —his real waking eyes, not his dream ones—sharply, and there he was, lying on the soft grass heap, not up in the sky among the cloud-children at all!

At first he was rather disappointed. But as he was thinking to himself whether it was worth while to try to go to sleep again and go on with his dream, he heard himself called as before, "Ted, *Ted*, TED."

And looking up he forgot all about everything else when he saw, running down the sloping banks as fast as his legs would carry him, Percy, his dear Percy!

Ted jumped up—even his wounded leg couldn't keep him still now.

"Was it thoo calling me, Percy?" he said. "I was d'eaming, do thoo know—*such* a funny d'eam? But I'm so glad thoo's come back, Percy. Oh, Ted *is* so glad."

Then all the day's adventures had to be related—the accident with the scissors and the drive in the wheelbarrow, and the funny dream. And in his turn Percy had to tell of all he had seen and done and heard—the shops he had been at in the little town, and what he had had for luncheon and—and—the numberless trifles that make up the interest of a child's day.

"Does thoo think there's any shop where we could get *wings*, Percy?" asked Ted. He had the vaguest ideas as to what "shops" were, but Percy had been telling him of the beautiful little boats he had seen

at a toy-shop in the market-place, "boats with white
sails and all rigged just like real ones ;" and if boats
with white sails were to be got, why not white wings ?

"Wings !" exclaimed Percy.   "What sort of wings
do you mean, Teddy ?"

"Wings for little boys," Ted explained.   "Like
what I was d'eaming about.   It would be so nice to
fly, Percy."

"Beautiful, wouldn't it ?" agreed Percy.   But nobody can fly, Ted.   Nobody *could* make wings that
would be any use for people.   People can't fly."

"But little boys, Percy," persisted Ted.   "Little
boys isn't so very much bigger than birds.   Oh, you
don't know how *lovely* it feels to fly.   Percy, *do* let
us try to make some wings."

But Percy's greater experience was less hopeful.

"I'm afraid it would be no use," he said.   "People
have often tried.   I've heard stories of it.   They
only tumbled down."

"Did they hurt themselves ?" asked Ted.

"I expect so," Percy replied.

Just then David, who was passing by, stopped to
tell the boys that some one was calling them in from
the house.

"Is it your papa, Master Ted ; yes, I think," he said.

Ted's leg was feeling less stiff and painful now. He could walk almost as well as usual. When they got to the house-door his father was waiting for him. He had heard of Ted's misfortune, and there was rather a comical smile on his face as he stooped to kiss his little boy.

"I want you to come in to see Mr. Brand," he said. "He says he hasn't seen you for a long time, little Ted."

Ted raised his blue eyes to his father's face with a rather puzzled expression.

"Whom's Mr. Brand?" he asked.

"Why, don't you remember him, Teddy?" said Percy. "That great big gentleman—so awfully tall."

Ted did not reply, but he seemed much impressed.

"Is him a diant?" he asked, gravely.

"Very nearly, I should say," said Percy, laughing, and then, as he had already seen Mr. Brand, who had met Ted's father on his way back from A——, Percy ran off in another direction, and Ted followed his father into the drawing-room.

Mr. Brand was sitting talking to Ted's mother, but just as the door opened, he rose from his seat and came forward.

"I was just going to ask you if—ah! here's your

E

little boy," he said to Ted's father. Then, sitting down again, he drew Ted between his knees and looked kindly at the small innocent face. He was very fond of children, but he did not know much about them, and Ted, looking and feeling rather over-awed, stood more silently than usual, staring seriously at the visitor.

He was very tall and very big. Whether he quite came up to Ted's idea of a "diant" I cannot tell. But queer fancies began to chase each other round the boy's brain. There had been a good deal to excite and upset the little fellow—at no time a strong child —that day, and his dream when lying asleep on the grass had added to it all. And now, as he stood look-ing up at big Mr. Brand, a strange confusion of ideas filled his mind—of giants tall enough to reach the sky, to catch and bring down some of the cloud-wings Ted wished so for, interspersed with wondering if it was "fissy oil" that had made this big man so very big. If he, Ted, were to take a great, great lot of fissy oil, would *he* grow as big and strong? Would he be able to cut the grass like David perhaps, to run faster than Percy—to—to I don't know what—for at this moment Mr. Brand's voice brought him back from his fancies.

"What an absent-minded little fellow he is," Mr. Brand was saying, for he had been speaking to Ted two or three times without the child's paying any attention.

"Not generally," said Ted's mother. "He is usually very wide-awake to all that is going on. What are you thinking of, Ted, dear?"

"Yes," said Mr. Brand. "Tell us what you've got in your head. Are you thinking that I'm a very tiny little man — the tiniest little man you ever saw?"

"No," said Ted solemnly, without the least smile, at which his mother was rather surprised. For, young though he was, Ted was usually very quick at seeing a joke. But he just said "No," and stared again at Mr. Brand, without another word.

"Then what were you thinking—that I'm the very *biggest* man you ever did see?"

"Ses," said Ted, gravely still, but with a certain light in his eyes which encouraged Mr. Brand to continue his questions.

"And what more? Were you wishing you were as big as I am?"

Ted hesitated.

"I'd *rather* fly," he said. "But Percy says nobody

can fly. I'd like to be big if I could get up very high."

"How high?" said Mr. Brand. "Up to the top of the mountain out there?"

"Is the mountain as high as the clouds?" asked Ted.

"Yes," said Mr. Brand; "when you're up at the very top, you can look down on the clouds."

Ted looked rather puzzled.

"I'll tell you what," the gentleman went on, amused by the expression of the child's face, "I'll tell you what—as I'm so big, supposing I take you to the top of the mountain—we'll go this very afternoon. I'll take a jug of cold water and a loaf of bread, and leave it with you there so that you'll have something to eat, and then you can stay there quite comfortable by yourself and find out all you want to know. You'd like that, wouldn't you? to be all by yourself on the top of the mountain?"

He looked at Ted in a rather queer way as he said it. The truth was that Mr. Brand, who though so big was not very old, was carried away by the fun (to *him*) of watching the puzzled look on the child's face, and forgot that what to him was a mere passing joke might be very different to the tender little four-years-old boy.

Ted's face grew rather white, he edged away a little from this strange gentleman, whom he could not make out, but who was so big that Ted felt it impossible to doubt his being able to do anything he wished.

"You'd like that, wouldn't you?" he repeated, quite gravely, and glancing at Ted with slightly knitted brows which made the boy suddenly think of some of the "ogre" stories he had heard.

"No," said Ted bluntly. But he was afraid to say more. Ogres didn't like to be contradicted, and perhaps—*perhaps* this strange man really thought he *would* like it, and really meant to please him. Any way, it would never do to answer rudely, though Ted's face grew still paler, when his glance fell on the mountain peak clearly to be seen out of the window from where he stood, and a little shiver ran through him when he thought that perhaps he would have to go, whether he liked it or not. He edged away still farther, but it was no use. Mr. Brand had put his arm round him, and there was no getting away, when suddenly a noise outside the window caught the gentleman's attention and he started up. It was his dog barking loudly, and Mr. Brand, fearing he might have got into some mischief, stepped out through the glass door to see. Ted was on the alert, and before any one in the room had noticed him he was off.

Where should he go to? He dared not hide in the garden, for there he might be seen, especially as Mr. Brand was running about after his dog; he would not go up to the nursery, for nurse would ask him why he had not stayed downstairs; he did not even wish to find Percy, for though he could not have explained why, he felt that it would be impossible for him to tell *any one* of the strange terror that Mr. Brand's joke had awakened. He felt ashamed of it, afraid too that if, as he vaguely thought might be the case, the offer had been made in real earnest and with a wish to please him, his dislike to it would be ungrateful and unkind. Indeed poor Ted was more troubled than he ever remembered to have been in his whole little life—he could think of nothing for it but to hide till all danger was past.

A brilliant idea struck him—he would go and pay a visit to cook! It was not very often he went into the kitchen, and no one would look for him there. And cook was kind, very kind when not very busy. So with a slight shudder as, running past the open front-door, he caught sight of the well-known mountain peak, frowning at him, as it seemed now, for the first time in his life, Ted made his way to cook's quarters.

She was not in the kitchen, but hearing some one coming, she called out from the back kitchen where she was. That was better still, every step the farther from the drawing-room, or from Mr. Brand rather, was a gain. So Ted trotted into the back kitchen, and to prevent cook's thinking there was anything the matter asked her if he might play with the cat. He found a piece of string, to which cook tied a cork, and as pussy was really more of a kitten than a cat, he amused himself for some time by making her run after it, whistling now and then to keep up his heart, though had cook looked at him closely she could have seen how white he was, and how every now and then he threw frightened glances over his shoulder.

" Your leg's better, Master Ted ?" said cook.

" Oh ses, zank thoo," said Ted. " Him's much better."

" You'll have to take care never to touch sharp tools again, won't you ?" she went on, as she bustled about with her work.

" Ses," he said again. But he did not speak with his usual heartiness, and cook, who, like all the servants, loved the bright, gentle little fellow, looked at him rather anxiously. Suddenly a sound was heard—wheels on the gravel drive.

"What's that, cook?" said Ted, starting.

"Only the gentleman's dog-cart—the gentleman that's been to see your papa. He's going away," said cook composedly.

Ted hurried into the kitchen. From the window the drive could be seen by big people, though not by him.

"Lift me up on the table, please, cook," he said, and when cook good-naturedly did so, and he saw the giant really, actually driving away, Ted could almost have cried with pleasure. But his fears and his relief he kept in his own little heart.

"Zank thoo, cook," he said gravely, but with the pretty courtesy he never forgot. "Zank thoo, and please lift me down again."

"He's a funny little fellow," said cook to herself, as she watched Ted trot off. "I wonder what he'd got in his mind, bless him."

Ted reappeared in the drawing-room.

"Where have you been, dear?" said his mother. "We were looking about for you to say good-bye to Mr. Brand. Where did you go to?"

"Ted were in the kitchen, 'peaking to cook," he replied.

"But why did you go away, dear, while Mr. Brand was here?" asked his mother. "Were you frightened of his dog?"

"No," said Ted, "Ted's never frightened of dogs."

"No, dear, I know you're not," said his mother. But she did not feel satisfied. Her little boy did not look the same as usual somehow. Still she felt it was better to ask no more—after a while Ted would perhaps tell her of himself. And she did well, for it would have been almost impossible for him to tell his mingled feelings.

"Muzzer likes that big man," he was thinking to himself. "Muzzer thinks he's kind. It's naughty and unkind of Ted to be frightened," and so the loyal little man kept silence.

And it was not for a long time—not till Ted himself had learnt to "understand" a little better, that even his mother understood the whole.

CHAPTER IV.

THE STORY OF SUNNY.

" Of course he was the giant,
With beard as white as snow."

BUT whenever Mr. Brand, poor man, came to call, Ted was sure in some mysterious way to disappear. After a while his mother began to notice it, though, as Mr. Brand did not come very often, she did not do so all at once. She noticed, however, another thing which she was sorry for. Ted took a dislike to the big mountain. It was a great pity, for before that he had been so fond of it—so fond of watching the different expressions, "looks" Ted called them, that it wore according to the time of day, or the time of year, or the weather. And his father and mother had been pleased to see him so "noticing," for such a little boy; they thought it showed, as indeed it did, that he was likely to grow into a happy-minded and happy-hearted man.

But now it was quite different. When he sat on his mother's knee in the drawing-room he would turn his little face to the side away from the window so that he should not see the towering mountain-head. He would never laugh at his old friend's putting on his nightcap of mist, as he used to do, and all his pretty fancies about being able to reach the dear little stars if he were up on the top peak of all, were spoilt.

"Something has frightened Ted," said his mother to his father one day. "I wonder what it can be. I know *you* wouldn't frighten him, dear," she added, turning to Percy who was in the room, though of course *Ted* was not there, otherwise his mother would not have said it, "but still, has there been anything in your play that could have done so? Have you been talking about mountains, or telling stories about them?"

"No," said Percy, thoughtfully; "I'm sure there has been nothing. Shall I ask Ted about it? Perhaps he wouldn't mind telling me, not even as much as——" Percy stopped and grew a little red. He was a boy of nice feelings, not rough and knock-about in his ways like many schoolboys.

"Not even as much as telling *me*, you were going

to say," said Ted's mother, smiling. "Never mind, dear. I daresay it *would* be easier for him to tell you, and I am very glad my little boy has such a kind Percy to talk to. But I think perhaps it is better to say nothing to him. We may find it out by degrees, and if it is only a sort of fancy—he may have seen the mountain looking gloomy some evening—it may fade away of itself more quickly if we don't notice it."

That day was a very bright and lovely one. Ted's mother thought to herself she would like to do something to make Ted, and Percy too, "extra" happy, for the weeks had been running on fast—it would soon be time for Percy, not being a little fish, to go back to school. And Percy's big sister was with them too just then. She was even bigger than Percy, so of course Ted thought her *quite* grown up, though in reality she was a good many years off being so. She was very nice any way, with a gentle pretty face and kind eyes, and though she was not very old she was very clever at telling stories, which is a most delightful thing in a big sister or cousin—is it not? And she was also able to sing very prettily, another delightful thing, or at least so Ted thought, for he *was* so fond of singing. This big girl's name was Mabel.

And after thinking a while and talking about it to Mabel, Ted's mother thought the nicest thing would be to have tea in a lonely little nesty place in the gorge between the mountains that I have told you of. We were to go there with Ted and Cheviott some day, by the by, were we not? Well, never mind, Cheviott shall be—that is to say he *was*—of the gipsy tea-party, so that will come to the same thing, will it not?

They all set off—Ted's father and mother, another gentleman and lady who were staying for the summer in a cottage not far off, that they might be near their friends, their daughter who was *really* grown up, and Mabel and Percy and Ted. You can fancy the bread and butter there was to cut, the home-made cake, the tea and sugar and cream that must not be forgotten. And when all the baskets were ready and everybody was helping and planning how to carry them, who do you think got hold of the biggest of all and was trying to lug it along? Who but our four-years-old Ted?

"My boy, my boy," cried his mother, laughing, for he did look comical—the basket being really very nearly as big as himself and his little face already quite red with the exertion, "you cannot possibly take that basket. Why, *I* could scarcely carry it."

"But boys is stronger than muzzers," said Ted
gravely, and it was really with difficulty that they
could persuade him to give it up, and only then by
letting him carry another which *looked* nearly as
important but was in reality much lighter, as it only
held the tablecloth and the teapot and teaspoons.

I have not told you about the gorge—not told you,
I mean, how lovely it was. Nor if I talked about it
for hours could I half describe its beauty. In spring
time perhaps it was the prettiest of all, for then it
was rich in the early blossoms and flowers that are
so quickly over, and that seem to us doubly precious
after the flower famine of the winter. But not even
in the early spring time, with all the beauty of primroses and violets, could the gorge look lovelier than
it did this summer afternoon. For the ferns and
bracken never seemed dusty and withered in this
favoured place—the grass and moss too, kept their
freshness through all the hot days as if tended by
fairy fingers. It was thanks to the river you see—
the merry beautiful little river that came dancing
down the centre of this mountain-pass, at one part
turning itself into a waterfall, then, as if tired, for a
little flowing along more quietly through a short
space of less precipitous road. But always beautiful,

always kindly and generous to the happy dwellers on
its banks, keeping them cool in the hottest days,
tossing here and there its spray of pearly drops as if
in pretty fun.

On each side of the water ran a little footpath,
and here and there roughly-made rustic bridges across
it tempted you to see if the other side was as pretty
as this, though when you had stood still to consider
about it you found it impossible to say! The paths
were here and there almost completely hidden, for
they were so little trodden that the moss had it all its
own way with them, and sometimes too it took a
scramble and a climb to fight one's way through the
tangled knots and fallen fragments of rock which
encumbered them. But now and then there came a
bit of level ground where the gorge widened slightly,
and then the path stopped for a while in a sort of
glade from which again it emerged on the other side.
It was in one of these glades that Ted's mother
arranged the gipsy tea. Can you imagine a prettier
place for a summer day's treat? Overhead the bluest
of blue skies and sunshine, tempered by the leafy
screen-work of the thickly growing trees; at one side
the soft rush of the silvery river, whose song was here
low and gentle, though one could hear in the distance

the boom of the noisy waterfall; at the other side the mountain slope, whose short brown slippery turf seemed to tempt one to a climb. And close at hand the wealth of ferns and bracken and flowers that I have told you of—a little higher up strange gleaming balls of many kinds of fungus, yellow and orange, and even scarlet, flamed out as if to rival the softer tints of the trailing honeysuckle and delicate convolvulus and pink foxglove below. It was a lovely dream of fairyland, and the knowing that not far away the waves of the broad blue sea were gently lapping the sandy shore seemed somehow to make it feel all the lovelier.

The tea of course was a great success—when was a gipsy tea, unless people are *very* cross-tempered and fidgety and difficult to please, anything else? The kettle did its duty well, for the water boiled in it beautifully on the fire of dry sticks and leaves which Percy and Mabel, and busy Ted *of course,* had collected. The tea tasted very good—"not 'moky at all," said Ted; the slices of bread and butter and cake disappeared in a wonderful way, till at last everybody said "No, thank you, not any more," when the boys handed round the few disconsolate-looking pieces that remained.

And after this there was the fun of washing up
and packing away, in which Ted greatly distinguished
himself. Hs would not leave the least shred of paper
or even crumbs about, for the fairies would be angry,
he said, if their pretty house wasn't left "kite tidy."
And Percy and Mabel were amused at his fancy, and
naturally enough it set them talking about fairies and
such like. For the children were by themselves now
—the ladies had gone on a little farther to a place
where Ted's mother wanted to sketch, and the gentlemen had set off to climb to the nearest peak, from
whence there was a beautiful view of the sea. It
would have been too much for Ted, and indeed when
his father had asked him if he would like to go part
of the way with them, both his mother and Percy
. noticed that a troubled look came over his happy face,
as he said he would rather stay where he was, which
was strange for him, for though such a little boy, he
was always eager for a climb and anxious to do
whatever he saw any one else doing. So kind Percy,
mindful of Ted's mother's words, said he would not
go either, and stayed with the others, helping them to
tidy up the fairies' house.

"Now," said Ted at last, sitting down on the grass
at Mabel's feet, "now I *sink* the fairies will be p'eased.

F

It's all kite tidy. Fairies is always angry if peoples is untidy."

"I thought fairies were always in a good humour," said Percy. "I didn't know they were ever angry."

"Oh, I think Ted's right," said Mabel. "They are angry with people who are dirty or untidy. Don't you remember a story about them coming to work in a house where the kitchen was always left tidy at night? And they never would come to the next house because it was always in a mess."

"P'ease tell me that story, Mabel," said Ted.

"I'm afraid I don't remember it very well," she replied.

"Do you remember," said Percy, who was lying on the ground staring up at the sky and the bit of brown mountain peak that could be seen from where he was, "do you remember, Mab, the story of a little boy that fell asleep on the top of a mountain, and the fairies spirited him away, and took him down to their country, down inside the mountain? And he thought he had only been away—when he came home again, I mean, for they had to let him out again after a while—he thought he had only been away a day or two, and, fancy, it had been twenty years! All the children had grown big, and the young people middle-aged, and the middle-aged people quite old, and none of them knew him again. He had lost all his childhood. Wasn't it sad?"

"Yes, *very*," said Mabel; "I remember the story."

"I think it's dedful," said Ted. "I don't like mountains, and I don't like diants. I'll never go up a mountain, never."

"But it wasn't the mountain's fault, Ted," said Percy. "And it wasn't giants, it was fairies."

"I sink p'raps it was diants," persisted Ted. "I don't like zem. Mr. Brand is a diant," he added mysteriously, in a low voice.

Percy had been thinking of what Ted's mother had said. Now he felt sure that it was something to do with Mr. Brand that had frightened the little fellow. But Mabel did not know about it.

"I like mountains," she said. "Indeed I love them. I am always so glad to live where I can see their high peaks reaching up into the sky."

"But it wouldn't be nice to be alone, kite alone, on the top of one of zem, would it?" said Ted.

"No, it wouldn't be nice to be alone in any far-off place like that," said Percy, "but of course nobody would ever stay up on the top of a mountain alone."

"But if zem was *made* to," said Ted doubtfully.

" I wouldn't mind so much if I had Chevie," he added, putting his arm round the dear doggie's neck and leaning his little fair head on him, for of course Chevie was of the party.

" Poor Ted," said Percy, laughing. " No one would ever make *you* live up all alone on the top of a mountain. Mabel, I wish you'd tell us a story," he said to his sister. " It's so nice here. I shall go to sleep if somebody doesn't do something to keep me awake."

He was lying at full length on the soft mossy grass, in the same place still, and gazing up at the blue sky and brown mountain peak. " Tell us a story, Mab," he repeated lazily.

" I haven't got any very nice ones just now," said Mabel. " I have been so busy with my lessons, you know, Percy, that I haven't had time for any stories."

" Can't you make them up yourself ?" said Percy.

" Sometimes I do, a little," she replied. " But I can't make them all quite myself. Sometimes in our German reading-books there are funny little bits of stories, and I add on to them. There was one—oh yes, I'll tell you one about a giant who lived on the top of a mountain."

Ted drew nearer to Mabel, and nestled in to her side.

"A diant on the top of a mountain," he repeated. "Is it very f'ightening, Mabel?"

"Oh no. Listen and I'll tell you. Once, a long time ago, there was, a long way off, a strange country. There were lots and lots of forests in it, and at the side of the biggest forest of all there rose a chain of high mountains. The people who lived in this forest were poor, simple sort of people—they hadn't much time for anything but work, for it was difficult to gain enough to live on. Most of them were charcoal-burners, and there were not very many of them altogether. Of course in a forest there wouldn't be much room for cottages and houses, would there? And their cottages were none of them near together. Each family had its own hut, quite separated from the others, and unless you belonged to the forest you could hardly find your way from one part of it to the other. The poor people, too, were so busy that they had not much time for going to see each other, or for amusing themselves in any way. They all had a pale sad look, something like the look that I have heard papa say the poor people in some parts of England have—the people in those parts where they work so awfully hard in dark smoky towns and never see the sun, or the green fields, or anything fresh and pretty. Of course the forest people were not as badly off as *that*—for their work any way was in the open air, and the forest was clean—not like dirty factories, even though it was so dark. It was the want of sunshine that was their worst trouble, and that gave them that white, dull, half-frightened look. The forest was too thick and dense for the sun to get really into it, even in winter, and then, of course, the rays are so thin and pale that they aren't much good if they do come. And the mountains at the side came so close down to the edge of the forest that there was no getting any sunshine there either, for it was the north side there, the side that the sunshine couldn't get to. So for these reasons the place had come to be called 'the sunless country.'"

"What was there at the other side of the forest?" said Percy; "couldn't they have got into the sunshine at that side?"

"No," said Mabel. "I think there was a river or something. Or else it was that the forest was so very, very big that it would have been quite a journey to get out at any other side. I think that was it. Any way they couldn't. And they just had to live on without sunshine as well as they could. Their fathers had done so before them, and there was no help for it, they thought. They were too poor and too hard-worked to move away to another country, or to do anything but just go through each day as it came in a dull sad way, seldom speaking even to each other.

"But do you know, it had *not* always been so in the sunless forest, though the better times were so long ago that hardly any of the poor people knew it had ever been different. There had, once upon a time, been a way into the sunshine on the other side of the mountain, and this way lay right through the great hill itself. But the mountain belonged to a great and very powerful giant"—at this Ted edged still closer to Mabel—"who lived in it quite alone. Sometimes he used to come out at a hole in the top, which was his door, and stay up there for a while looking about him, staring at the black forest down at his feet, and smiling grimly to himself at the thought of how dark and dull it must be for the people who lived in it. For he was not a kind giant at all. It was he that had shut up the passage through which the poor forest people used to pass to their bright cottages on the other side. for in those days they didn't *live* in the forest, they only went there for their work, and on Sundays and holidays they were all happy and merry together, and the little children grew up rosy and bright, quite different from the poor little wan-faced creatures that now hung sadly about at the hut doors in the forest, looking as if they didn't know how to laugh or play."

"Why did the naughty diant shut up the way?" asked Ted.

"Because he had a quarrel with the forest people. He wanted them to let their little boys and girls, or some of them, come to him to be his servants, but they wouldn't, and so he was so angry that he shut up the door. But that was so long ago now that the people had almost forgotten about it—the children that the giant had wanted to be his servants were old grandfathers and grandmothers now, and some of them were dead, I daresay, so that the real history of their troubles was forgotten by them but not by the giant, for whenever he came out at the top of the mountain to take some air, he used to look down at the forest and think how dull and miserable they must be there."

"Nasty diant," said Ted.

"Yes, he was very unkind, but still I think you would have been rather sorry for him too. He was

old and all alone, and of course nobody loved him.
The people in the forest hardly ever spoke of him.
They knew he was there, or that he used to be there,
and now and then some of the children who had heard
about him used to feel afraid of him and whisper to
each other that he would eat them up if he could
catch them, but that was about all the notice they
took of him. They seemed to have forgotten that he
was the cause of their sad, gloomy lives, and indeed
I am not sure that any except some very old people
really knew. Among these very old people there
were a man and his wife who were almost the poorest
of all in the forest. They were so poor because they
were almost past work, and they had no children to
work for them. All that they had was a little grand-
daughter, who lived with them because her father and
mother were dead. And it was a queer thing that
she was quite different from the other poor children
in the forest. They were all pale and sad and crushed-
looking like their parents. This little girl was bright-
haired and bright-eyed and rosy-cheeked. She was
the one merry happy creature in the forest, and all
the poor people used to stand and look at her as she
flitted about, and wish that their children were the
same. I don't know what her real name was; the

story didn't tell, but the name she got to have among
the forest people was Sunshine—at least it was Sunshine in German, but I think 'Sunny' is a nicer
name, don't you ?"

"Yes," said Percy; and

"Ses," said Ted, "'Sunny' is nicest."

"Well, we'll call her 'Sunny.' The reason that
she was so different was partly that she hadn't been
born in the forest. Her father, who was the son of
these old people, had gone away, as some few of the
forest people did, to another country, and there he
had married a bright-haired, pretty girl. But she
had died, and he himself got very ill, and he had only
strength to bring his baby girl back to the forest to
his parents when he too died. So Sunny's history
had been rather sad, you see, but still it hadn't made
her sad—it seemed as if the sunshine was *in* her
somehow, and that nothing could send it away."

Mabel stopped. Voices and steps were heard
coming near.

"They're coming back," she said. "I'll have to
finish the story another time. I didn't think it
would take so long to tell."

"Oh *do* go on now, dear, dear Mabel, oh *do!*" cried
Ted beseechingly.

But Mabel's fair face grew red.

"I couldn't, Ted, dear," she said, "not before big people," and Percy sympathised with her.

"We'll hear the rest in the garden at home," he said.

"Thoo won't tell it without me, not without Ted, p'ease," asked the little fellow.

"No, no, of course not, darling," said Mabel as she kissed his eager face.

Just then a ray of bright evening sunshine fell on Ted's brown hair, lighting it up and deepening it to gold, and as the little fellow caught it in his eyes, he looked up laughing.

"There's Sunny kissing Ted too," he said merrily.

CHAPTER V.

THE STORY OF SUNNY (*Concluded*).

" A child of light, a radiant lass,
    And cheerful as the morning air."

THEY were all three laughing at Ted's wit when his mother and the other ladies came upon them.

" You seem very happy, children," said she.

" Oh ses," said Ted. " Mabel has been telling us such a lovely story. It's not finnied yet. She's going to tell the rest in the garden at home. Oh, I *am* so happy. It's been such a sprendid day."

He began half humming to himself in the excess of his delight.

" Ted wishes somebody would sing a song," he said.

His mother glanced at Mabel. Poor Mabel's face grew very red again. It would be worse than telling a story.

" If we all sang together," she said timidly, " I wouldn't mind trying to begin."

So in a minute or two her clear young voice sang out—like a lark's it seemed to mount higher and still higher, gathering strength and courage as it grew, and then softly dropping again as if to fetch the others, who joined her in the old familiar chorus of the simple song she had chosen—"Home, sweet home."

Ted listened entranced, and his little voice here and there could be distinguished. But suddenly, as Mabel stopped and a momentary silence fell on them all, he turned to his mother, and throwing himself into her arms, burst into tears.

"Muzzer," he said, "I can't bear it. It's *too* pitty," and though his mother and Mabel soothed the excited little fellow with gentle words and caresses, there were tears in more eyes than Ted's as they all thanked Mabel for her singing.

It was the next day that they had the rest of the story. The children were all in the garden together, not far from Ted's favourite "bridge." They could hear the babble of the little brook as it chattered past in the sunshine, and now and then the distant cry of a sea-bird would sound through the clear air, making Cheviott prick up his ears and look very wide-awake all of a sudden, though in reality, being no longer in the first bloom of youth, he was apt to get rather drowsy on a hot afternoon.

"We'se all ready, Mabel," said Ted, settling himself down comfortably in his favourite rest at her side. "Now go on p'ease. I can see the top of the mountain kite nice from here, and zen I can sink I'll see the old diant poking his head out," evidently the child's fear of the mountain was fast becoming a thing of the past, and Percy felt quite pleased.

"Well," began Mabel, "I was telling you that Sunny had lived with her old grandfather and grandmother since she was quite little. They were very kind to her, but they were very poor, almost the poorest of all in the forest. And yet their cottage never seemed quite so dull and sad as the others. How could it, when there was always Sunny's bright head flitting about, and her merry voice sounding like a bird's ?

" The old people looked at her half with pleasure and half sadly.

" ' It can't last,' the old man said one day, when the little girl was running and jumping about in her usual happy way.

" The old woman knew what he meant without his explaining, and she nodded her head sadly, and just then Sunny came flying into the cottage to show them some flowers she had actually found in the forest, which, you see, was the greatest wonder possible, for there were almost *never* any flowers to be seen. And Sunny told them how she had found them in a little corner where the trees did not grow quite so thick, so that more light could get in. And when she saw how surprised the old people were, she looked at them rather strangely, and some new thoughts seemed to be awaking in her mind, and she said, 'Grandfather, why aren't there more flowers in the forest, and why am I the only little girl that laughs and sings? Why does everybody look sad here? I can remember a little, just a little, about the other country I lived in before I came here. People used to laugh and smile there, and my mother had bright hair like mine, and father too was not sad till after mother had gone away and we came to this dark land. Why is it so dark, and why do you all look so sad?'

"The old man told her it was all for want of the sun, 'the blessed sun,' he called it, and Sunny thought about his words a great deal. And bit by bit she got the whole story from him, for he was one of the few remaining old people who knew the reason of their misfortunes. And Sunny thought and thought

it over so much that she began to leave off dancing
and laughing and singing as she used, so that her
poor grandfather and grandmother began to be afraid
that the sadness of the forest was at last spoiling her
happy nature, and for a while they were very sorry
about her. But one day she told them what she had
in her mind. This was what she said to them—

"'Dear grandfather and grandmother, I cannot
bear to see the sadness of the poor people here, and
I have been thinking if nothing can be done. And
a few nights ago I had a strange dream. I dreamt
that a beautiful lady stood beside me and said, 'Go,
Sunny, and have no fear. The giant will not harm
you.' And since then it has come into my mind that
I might win back the sunshine for our poor neighbours, and for you too, dear grandfather and grandmother, for you are not so very old yet, if you will
let me go to see if I can melt the giant's hard heart.'

"Sunny was standing in front of the old couple,
and as she spoke, to their amazement, a sudden ray of
sunshine crept in through the little rough window of
the cottage and fell softly on her bright head. Her
grandfather looked at her grandmother, and her grandmother looked at her grandfather. They didn't know
how to speak—they were so surprised. Never, since

they were quite, quite little children had they seen such a thing. And they whispered to each other that it must be a magic sign, they must let the child go. I think it was very good and kind of them to let her go, the only thing they had to cheer them. The tears rolled down their poor old faces as they said good-bye to her, not knowing if they would live to see her return. But they said to each other, 'We have not very many years to live. It would be very wrong of us to lose the chance of life and happiness for all the poor forest people just to keep *our* bit of sunshine to ourselves.' And so they let her go, for they were good old people."

"Ses," said Ted, "zem was very kind. But how dedful for Sunny to have to go to the diant. Did her go all alone, Mabel?"

"Yes, all alone. But she wasn't frightened. And somehow her grandfather and grandmother weren't frightened for her either. They had a feeling that she *had* to go, and so she did. She set off the very next morning. Her grandfather explained the way to her, for old as he was he had never forgotten the days when the passage through the giant's mountain was left free and open, so that there was no need for the forest people to spend all their lives in the gloom and shade.

G

"Sunny walked quietly along the dark paths among the trees. She didn't dance and skip as usual, for she felt as if all of a sudden she had grown almost into a woman, with the thought of what she had to do for her poor neighbours. And as she looked about her, she felt as if she had never before quite noticed how dark and chill and gloomy it was. She had a good way to walk, for since the closing of the passage the people had moved farther and farther into the forest. They had grown afraid of the giant, and were glad to get as far from him as they could, for there was no good to be got by staying near him. So Sunny walked on, past the cottages she knew, where she nodded to the people she saw, but without speaking to them, which was so unlike her usual merry way that they all looked after her in surprise and wondered what had come over the little girl. And one or two of them shook their heads and said sadly that she was getting to be like the rest of them. But Sunny walked on, farther and farther, now and then smiling quietly to herself, and her bright little head shining in the darkness almost as if the sun was lighting it up. She went a good way, but there was nothing new or different. It was always the dark forest and the gloomy trees. But at last she saw,

" She hunted about among the leaves and branches till she
found a little silver knob."—P. 83.

close to her, behind the trees, the dark sides of the great mountain, and she knew that she must be near the closed-up door."

" Oh !" said Ted, " wasn't her afraid of bears ? "

" No," said Mabel, " she wasn't afraid of anything. She went quietly up to the door and stood before it. It was barred and barred with iron, and it was so long since it had been opened that the ivy and those sorts of plants had grown all over it, creeping round the iron bars. It looked as if it hadn't been opened for a hundred years, and I daresay it hadn't been. But Sunny knew what to do. She hunted about among the leaves and branches till she found a little silver knob—her grandfather had told her about it; and the queer thing was that though the iron bars were quite rusted over so that you wouldn't have known what they were, the little silver knob was still bright and shining as if it had been cleaned every day always."

" Wif plate-powder," said Ted, who was very learned about such matters, as he was very fond of watching the servants at their work.

" Yes," said Mabel, " just as if it had been cleaned with plate-powder. Well, Sunny pressed this little knob, and a minute or two after she heard a clear tinkling bell. That was just what her grandfather had told her she would hear, so she stood quite still and waited. In a little while she seemed to hear a sound as of something coming along the passage, and suddenly the top part of the door—at least it was more like a window cut in the door—opened, and a voice, though she could not see anybody, called out, ' Have you come to stay ?' This too was what her grandfather had told her she would hear, so she knew what to say, and she answered ' Yes.' Then the voice said again, ' At what price ?' and Sunny answered, ' Sunshine for the forest.' But her heart began to beat faster when the door slowly opened and she saw that she must enter the dark passage. There was no one to be seen, even though the voice had sounded quite near, so Sunny just walked on, looking about her, for gradually as she went farther, either her eyes grew used to the darkness, or a slight light began to come, and in a few minutes she saw before her a very, very high staircase. It went straight up, without turnings or landings, and the steps were quite white, so she saw them plainly though the light was dim, and as there was nowhere else to go, she just went straight on. I can't tell you what a long time she seemed to keep going upstairs, but at last the steps stopped, and before her she saw another door. It wasn't a door like the one down below, it was more like a gate, for it was a sort of a grating that you could see through. Sunny pressed her face against it and peeped in. She saw a large dark room, with a rounded roof something like a church, and in one corner a very old, grim-looking man was sitting. He had a very long beard, but he didn't look so awfully big as Sunny had expected, for she knew he must be the giant. He was sitting quite still, and it seemed to Sunny that he was shivering. Any way he looked very old and very lonely and sad, and instead of feeling frightened of him the little girl felt very sorry for him. She stood there quite still, but though she didn't make the least noise he found out she was there. He waved his hand, and the barred door opened and Sunny walked in. She walked right up to the giant and made him a curtsey. Rather to her surprise he made her a bow, then he waved his hands about and moved his lips as if he were speaking, but no sound came, and Sunny stared at him in surprise. She began to wonder if he was deaf and dumb, and if so how could she explain to him what she had come for?

"'I can't understand what you are saying, sir,' she said very politely, and then, to her still greater surprise,

the waving of his hands and the moving of his lips
seemed to succeed, for in a very queer deep voice he
answered her.

"'What do you want?' he said. 'I sent my voice
downstairs to speak to you, and he has been loitering
on the way, lazy fellow, all this time. There are no
good servants to be had nowadays, none. I've not
had one worth his salt since I sent my old ones back'
to Ogreland when they got past work. What do you
want?'

"'Sunshine for the forest people.'

"That was all Sunny said, and she looked at the
grim old giant straight in the face. He looked at
her, and went on shivering and rubbing his hands.
Then he said, with a frown,

"'Why should they have sunshine? I can't get
it myself, since I'm too old to get up to the top there.
Sunshine indeed!' and then he suddenly stretched
out his hand to her and made a grab at her hair,
screaming out, 'Why, you've got sunshine! Come
here, and let me warm my hands. Ugh! that's the
first time I've felt a little less chilly these hundred
years,' and Sunny stood patiently beside him and
let him stroke her golden hair up and down, and in
a minute or two she said quietly,

" ' Will you unfasten the door, good Mr. Giant, and let the poor people through to the other side?'

" The giant still kept hold of her hair. ' It would be no good cutting it off—the sunshine would go out of it,' Sunny heard him saying to himself. So she just said again quietly, 'Will you unfasten the door, good Mr. Giant?'

"And at last he said, 'I'll consider about it. Your hair's getting cold. Go upstairs,' and he nodded his head towards a door in the corner of the room, ' go upstairs and fetch some sunshine for me, and come down again.'

"But Sunny wouldn't stir till she had got something out of him. And she said for the third time,

" ' Will you unfasten the door, good Mr. Giant, if I go upstairs to please you?'

" And the giant gave her a push, and said to her, 'Get off with you, you tiresome child. Yes, I'll open the door if you'll go and bathe your hair well, and then come down to warm my hands.'

So Sunny went upstairs. This stair wasn't like the other. It was a turny, screwy stair that went round and round itself, for you see it was near the top of the mountain and there wasn't so much room as down below. Sunny felt rather giddy when she

got to the top, but she got all right again in a minute
when she pushed open the little door she found there
and came out into the sunlight. It was *so* lovely,
and remember, she hadn't seen sunshine, even though
some of the brightness had stayed with her, since
she was a very little girl. You have no idea how
pretty it was up there, not gloomy at all, and with
the beautiful warm sunshine pouring down all round.
Sunny was very pleased to warm herself in it, and
then when she looked down over the side of the
mountain and saw the dark tops of the forest trees,
she was still more pleased to think that soon her poor
friends would have a chance of enjoying it too. And
when she thought that her hair had caught enough
sunshine to please the giant she called down through
the screwy staircase, 'Have you opened the door, Mr.
Giant ?' And when the giant said, 'Come down and
I'll tell you,' she answered, 'No, Mr. Giant, I can't
come till you've opened the door.' And then she
heard him grumbling to himself, and in a minute she
heard a rattling noise, and she knew the door was
opened, and then she came down. She had settled
with her grandfather that if she didn't come straight
back, he would send some of the people to watch for
the door being opened, so she knew it would be all

right, for once the giant had agreed to open it, he
couldn't shut it again—that was settled somehow,
some magic way I suppose, the story didn't say how.
So then Sunny came downstairs again, and the giant
stroked her hair up and down till his poor old hands
were quite warm, and he grew quite pleased and good-
natured. But he wouldn't let Sunny go away, and
she had to stay, you see, because the top-door, the one
like a gate, was still shut up. And any way she
didn't want to be unkind to the giant. She promised
him that she would come back to see him every day
if he liked if only he would let her go, but he wouldn't,
so she had to stay. I don't know how long she stayed.
It was a long time, for the story said she grew thin
and white with being shut up in the giant's cave and
having no running about. It was worse than the
forest. The only thing that kept her alive was the
sunshine she got every morning, for there was *always*
sunshine at the top of the mountain, and then, too, the
comfort of knowing that the poor people were enjoying it too, for when she was up on the top she could
hear their voices down below, as they came to the
door. Day by day she heard their voices grow merrier
and brighter, and after a while she could even hear
the little children laughing and shouting with glee.

And Sunny felt that she didn't mind for herself, she was *so* glad to think that she had done some good to her poor friends. But she got paler and thinner and weaker—it was so very tiring to stand such a long time every day while the giant stroked the sunshine out of her golden hair to warm his withered old hands, and it was so terribly dark and dull and cold in the gloomy cavern. She would hardly have known how the days went or when was day and when was night, but for the giant sending her upstairs every morning. But one morning came when she could not go; she got up a few steps, and then her strength went away and she seemed to get half asleep, and she said to herself that she was going to die, and she did not know anything more. She seemed to be dreaming. She fancied the giant came to look for her, and that his old face grew sad and sorry when he saw her. And then she thought she heard him say, 'Poor little girl, I did not mean to hurt her. I have done harm enough. Sunny, forgive me. The giant will do you and your people no more harm. His day is over.' Then she really did sleep, for a long time I fancy, for when she woke up she could not think where she was. She thought at first she was on the top of the mountain, it seemed so beautifully bright and warm. She sat up a little and looked about her, and she *couldn't* think where she was, for on one side close to her, she saw the dark trees of the forest that she knew so well, and on the other, smiling green fields and orchards and cottages with gardens filled with flowers, just the sort of country her grandfather had told her he remembered when he was a child on the other side of the great hill. It was just as if the mountain had melted away. And, just fancy, that *was* what had happened! For in a little while Sunny heard voices coming near her, all talking eagerly. It was the people of the forest who had found out what had come to pass, and they were all hurrying to look for Sunny, for they were terribly afraid that the giant had taken her away to Ogreland with the mountain. But he hadn't, you see! And Sunny and all the forest people lived all their lives as happy as could be—they were happier even than in the old days the grandfather and grandmother remembered, for not only were they free to leave the dark forest and enjoy the sunlight as often as they liked, but the sunshine now found its way by all the chinks and crannies among the branches into the very forest itself."

"And did they never hear anything more of the giant?" asked Percy.

"No," said Mabel, "only in hot summer days some-times, when the sun was beating down too much on the fields and gardens, the people of that country used to notice a large soft gray cloud that often came between them and the sunshine, and would stay there till the great heat grew less. This cloud seemed always the same shape, and somehow, Sunny, remem-bering her vision of the giant, thought to herself that the cloud was perhaps he, and that he wanted to make up for his long cruelty. And the children of the forest having heard her story used to laugh when they saw the cloud, and say to each other, 'See, there is the giant warming his hands.' But Sunny would say softly in a whisper, 'Thank you, Mr. Giant.'

"And though it is a very, very long time since all that happened, it has never been quite forgotten, and the people of that country are noted for their healthy happy faces, and the little children for their rosy cheeks and golden hair."

Mabel stopped.

"It is a very pretty story," said Percy. "Are there more like it in the book where you read it?"

Mabel was just going to answer, when her atten-tion was caught by Ted.

"I do believe he's asleep," she said softly, for Ted

had curled himself up like a dormouse in his little nest at her side. But just then the two-legged dormouse gave a funny chuckle, which showed that whether he *had* been asleep or not, he certainly was so no longer.

"What are you laughing at, Teddy?" said Percy.

"I were just sinking," said Ted, "what a silly boy Ted were to be afraid of mountains —— Ted would like to go up to the very, very top," he went on valorously. "Ted wouldn't mind a bit—not," with a prudent reservation, "not if thoo and Mabel was wif me."

CHAPTER VI.

LITTLE NARCISSA.

" But, I think, of all new-comers
Little children are the best."

FROM this time, I think, Ted lost his fear of mountains and giants. It was not till a long time afterwards that he explained to his mother exactly how it had been, and by that time he was of course quite big enough to understand that Mr. Brand had only been joking. But still he did not much care about seeing that gentleman again. He generally managed to be out of the way when he saw the dog-cart with the gray horse driving in at the gate, and just once, when he would not have had time to run off without actual rudeness, which little Ted *never* was guilty of, he only waited to shake hands and say "Quite well, thank thoo," before he disappeared in so unaccountable a manner that he could not be found as long as Mr. Brand's visit lasted.

It was a good deal thanks to Mabel's story that he grew to like his old friend the mountain again. But partly too, I daresay, he forgot his fears on account of several very interesting things that happened about this time. It was a great sorrow to him when Percy had to go back to school—that was one of little Ted's lasting or rather returning sorrows, all through his childhood. Only, like many things in our lives, if we learn to look at them in the right way, it was certainly a trouble with a bright side to it, a cloud with a silver lining—a silver lining which shone indeed all the brighter for the gray outside—for was there not the delight, the *delicious* delight, of the coming back again, the showing all the changes in the garden since Percy was last there, the new toys and other little presents that Ted had received, and listening to Percy's thrilling accounts of school-life, the relating his own adventures ?

Still there were times, especially now that Ted was really growing very sensible, that he wished for some other companion in his simple daily life, some one who, like the little fishes, did not have to go to school. And now and then, when, in his rare expeditions to the sea-side town not far off, he saw little groups of brothers and sisters trotting along together,

or when in the stories his mother read to him he heard
of happy nursery parties, Ted used to wish *he* had a
little "bruvver or sister, even a baby one would be
very nice." For deep down in his loving heart there
was already the true manly spirit, the longing to have
something to take care of and protect; something
tinier and more tender even than wee Ted himself.

And to make his child-life complete this pretty
thing came to him. With the autumn days, just
when Ted was beginning to feel a little sad at the
summer brightness going away, and his garden work
had come to be chiefly helping old David to sweep up
the fast-falling leaves, there came to Ted a dear little
baby sister. She was the dearest little thing—bright-
eyed and merry, and looking as if she was ready for
all sorts of fun. She was stronger than Ted had been,
and to tell the truth I think I must say prettier.
For sweet and fair and dear as was Ted's face both in
baby- and boy-hood, he was not what one would call
pretty. Not the sort of child whose proud nurse
comes home with wonderful stories of ladies stopping
her in the street to ask whose beautiful baby he was—
not 'a splendidly vigorous, stalwart little man like a
small eight-years-old of my acquaintance whose
mother was lately afraid to walk about the streets of

Berlin with him lest the old Emperor, as he sometimes does, should want to have him to make an officer of! No; Ted, though lithe and active as a squirrel, merry as a cricket, was not a "showy" child. He was just our own dear little Ted, our happy-hearted Christmas child.

But I suppose there never was in this world any one so happy but that it was *possible* for him to be happier. And this "more happiness" came to Ted in the shape of his baby sister, Narcissa. Boys who despise sisters, "girls" in any shape, big or little, don't know what a great deal they lose. Ted was still a good way off the "big boy" stage, and indeed I don't think anything could have made it possible for him to look at things as too many big boys do. By the time he reached schoolboy-hood, Narcissa was a dainty maiden of five or six, and quite able to stand up for herself in a little queenly way, even had her brother been less tender and devoted. And of the years between, though I would like to tell you something, I cannot tell you half nor a quarter. They were happy sunny years, though not *quite* without clouds of course. And the first summer of little Cissy's life was a sort of bright opening to them.

It was again a very beautiful summer. The

H

children almost lived out-of-doors. Poor nurse found
it difficult to get the work in the house that fell to
her share finished in the morning before Ted was
tugging at her to "tum out into the garden, baby
does *so* want to tum;" and baby soon learnt to clap
her hands and chuckle with glee when her little hat
was tied on and she was carried downstairs to her
perambulator waiting at the door. And there was
new interest for Ted in hunting for the loveliest wild
flowers he could find, as baby showed, or Ted *thought*
she did, a quite extraordinary love for the bouquets
her little brother arranged for her.

"Her knows *kite* well which is the prettiest ones,
doesn't her, nurse?" he said one day when they were
all three—all four rather, for of course Chevie was
one of the group—established in their favourite place
under the shade of a great tree, whose waving
branches little Cissy loved so much that she would
cry when nurse wheeled her away from it. "I think
baby knows *lots*, though she can't speak;" and baby,
pleased at his evidently talking of *her*, burst into a
funny crowing laugh, which seemed exactly as if
she knew and approved of what he was saying.

"Baby's a darling," said nurse.

"How soon will her learn to speak?" Ted inquired
gravely.

" Baby showed, or Ted *thought* she did, a quite extraordinary love for
the bouquets her little brother arranged for her."—P. 98.

"Not just yet. She hasn't got any teeth. Nobody can speak without teeth," said nurse.

"I hope," said Ted, more gravely still, "I hope Dod hasn't forgotten them."

Nurse turned away to hide a smile.

"No fear, Master Ted," she said in a minute. "She'll have nice little teeth by and by, you'll see. They'll be wee tiny white specks at first, and then they'll grow quite big and strong enough to bite with. That's how your teeth came. Not all of a sudden, you see."

"Ses," said Ted. "Nothing comes all in one sudden. The f'owers is weeny, weeny buds at first, and then they gets big. Nurse, I'm going to take my cart to get a *lot* of daisies down by the brook for baby. She likes to roll zem in her hands," and off he set with his little blue cart and white horse, his best beloved possession, and which had done good service in its time, to fill it with flowers for Cissy.

A few minutes later, as he was manfully dragging the cart up the path again, gee-upping and gee-whoing at the horse, which was supposed to find the daisy heads a heavy load uphill, his mother came out to the garden.

"Ted, dear," she said, "your father is going to

drive me to A——.　It is a long time since you were there, and I should like to have my little boy to go about with me while your papa is busy.　I have a good deal of shopping to do.　Would you like to go with me?"

Ted gave a shout of pleasure.　Then suddenly his glance fell on the little sister still in her perambulator under the big tree, and his eyes filled with tears.

"I would like dedfully to go," he said, "but poor Cissy.　I is *so* afraid Cissy will cry if I go."

He lifted his wistful little face to his mother's with an expression that went to her heart.

"Dear Ted," she said; "you are a good, kind, little boy.　But don't make yourself unhappy about Cissy. She is too little to cry for your going away, though she will laugh to see you come back."

Ted's face cleared, but suddenly a rosy colour spread over it.

"Muzzer," he said, in a low voice, tugging gently at her dress to make her stoop down, "muzzer, I *sink* I were going to cry not all for poor baby being sorry, but part 'cos I did so want to go."

Mother understood his simple confession.

"Yes, dear," she said, "I daresay you did, and it is right of you to tell me.　My good little Ted," she could not resist adding again, and again little Ted's face grew red, but this time with pleasure at mother's praise.

Baby bore the announcement, which he considered it his duty to make to her with great formality, very philosophically. Less philosophically did she take nurse's wheeling her away from under her beloved tree with its fluttering branches, towards the house, where nurse had to go to prepare Ted for his expedition. In fact, I am sorry to say that so little did the young lady realise what was expected of her, that she burst into a loud roar, which was quite too much for Ted's feelings.

"Dear baby, sweet baby," he cried, "thoo mustn't be tooked away from thoo's tree. I'll ask muzzer to deck me, nurse," he went on eagerly, for his mother had returned to the house, "or I can nearly kite well deck myself. I'll call thoo if I can't find my things. I'll run and ask muzzer," and off he went, so eager to give no trouble, so ready and helpful that nurse thought it best to let him have his way, and to devote her attention to the discomposed Miss Baby.

Ted did not find his mother quite so quickly as he expected, though he peeped into the drawing-room and called her by name as he passed her own room upstairs, on his way to the nursery. The fact was that mother was in the kitchen consulting with cook as to the groceries required to be ordered, and it never came into Ted's head to look for her there at this time of day. So he went straight on to the nursery, and managing with a good deal of tugging and pulling and coaxing to open *his* drawer in the chest, he got out his best little coat and hat and prepared to don them. But first he looked at his hands, which were none the whiter for their recent ravages among the daisies.

" Zem's very dirty," he said to himself; " zem must be washed."

There was water in the jug, but Ted's ambition was aroused, and great things were to be expected of a little boy who was big enough to "deck himself," as he would have described the process.

" Ses, zem's *very* dirty," he repeated, contemplating the two sunburnt little paws in question. " Zem should have hot water. Hot water makes zem ze most clean."

He glanced round, the hot water was not far to seek, for, though it was June, the weather was not very warm, and nurse generally kept a small fire burning in the day-nursery. And beside the fire, temptingly beside the fire, stood the kettle, into which Ted peeping, satisfied himself that there was water enough for his purpose. He would hardly have had patience to fetch it had it not been there, so eager was he for the delights of putting it on to boil. And, wonderful to say, he managed it; he got the kettle, heavy for him to lift, as you can imagine, safely on to the fire, and then, with immense satisfaction, sat down in front of it to watch the result. There was very little water in the kettle, but, though Ted did not think about that, it was all the less trying for his patience. And I hardly think either, that the water could have been quite cold in the first place, or else the fairies came down the chimney and blew up the fire with their invisible bellows to help little Ted, for certainly the kettle began to boil amazingly soon—first it simmered gently and then it began to sing more loudly, and at last what Ted called " moke " began to come out of the spout, and he knew that the kettle was boiling.

Ted was so used to hear nurse talking about the kettle " boiling" for tea, that it never came into his head that it was not necessary to have " boiling " water to wash his poor little hands. I don't indeed know what might not have happened to the whole of his poor little body had not his mother at that moment come into the room. A queer sight met her eyes— there was Ted, more than half undressed, barefooted and red-faced, in the act of lifting off the steaming kettle, round the handle of which, with wonderful precaution, he had wrapped his pocket-handkerchief.

Ted's mother kept her presence of mind. She did not speak till the kettle was safely landed on the floor, and Ted, with a sigh of relief, looked up and saw her at the door.

"I is decking myself, muzzer," he said with a pleased smile, and a charming air of importance, "Poor baby cried, so I told nurse I would deck myself, and nurse didn't mind."

"*Didn't* she?" said his mother, rather surprised.

"Oh, she thoughtened p'raps I'd find thoo, I amember," Ted continued, correcting himself.

"But did nurse know you were going to boil water?" said his mother.

"Oh no," said Ted, "it were only that my hands is *so* dirty. Zem needs hot water to make zem clean."

"Hot water, but not *boiling*," said his mother; "my dear little boy, do you know you might have scalded yourself dreadfully?"

"I put my hankerwick not to burn my hands," said Ted, rather disconsolately.

"Yes, dear. I know you meant it for the best, but just think if you had dropped the kettle and burnt yourself. And nurse has always told you not to play with fire or hot water."

"Ses," said Ted, "but I weren't *playing*. I were going to wash my hands to be nice to go out wif thoo," and his blue eyes filled with tears. But they were soon wiped away, and when his mother had with the help of *some* of the hot water made face and hands as clean as could be, and smoothed the tangled curls and fastened the best little coat, Ted looked very "nice" indeed, I can assure you, for his drive to A——.

It was a very happy drive. Perched safely between his father and mother, Ted was as proud as a king. It was all so pretty, the driving through the shady lanes, where the honeysuckle and wild-roses were just beginning to show some tints of colour, the peeps now and then of the sea below in its blue beauty, the glancing up sometimes at the mountain top, Ted's old friend, along whose sides they were actually travelling—it was all delightful. And when they drew near the little town, and the houses began to stand closer, till at last they came in rows and streets, and the old mare's hoofs clattered over the stones of the market-place so that the people in the sleepy little place came out to see who was coming, Ted's excitement knew no bounds. He had almost forgotten A——, it was so long since he had been there—the sights of the shops and what appeared to him their wonderful contents, the sight even of so many people and children walking about, was almost too much for the little country child; it seemed to take his breath away.

He recovered his composure, however, when he found himself trotting about the streets with his mother. She had several shops to go to, each, to Ted, more interesting than the other. There was the ironmonger's to visit, for cook had begged for a new preserving pan and the nursery tea-pot handle was broken; there were various milk jugs and plates to replace at the china shop; brown holland to get at the draper's for Ted's summer blouses. At two or three of the shops his mother, being a regular customer and having an account with them, did not pay, and among these was the grocer's, where she had rather a long list of things needed for the store-closet, and while she was explaining about them all to the white-aproned young man behind the counter, Ted marched about the shop on a voyage of discovery on his own account. There were so many interesting things— barrels of sugar, white, brown, and darker brown still, neat piles of raisins and currants, closely fastened bottles of French plums, and rows of paper-covered tin boxes which Ted knew contained biscuits.

"What a kind man," he said to himself, "to give muzzer all she wants," as one after another of his mother's requests was attended to. "Why, he lets muzzer take whatever her likes!" he added, as having brought his wanderings to a close for a minute, he stood beside her and saw her lifting a little square of honey soap out of a box which the grocer presented to her for examination, and, greatly impressed, Ted set off again on another ramble. Doubtless he too might take whatever he liked, and as the thought occurred to him he pulled up before another barrel filled with lumps, little and big, of half clear, whitey-looking stuff, something like very coarse lump sugar, only not *so* white, and more transparent. Ted knew what it was. It was soda, *washing* soda I believe it is usually called. Ted was, as I have said, very wide-awake about all household matters, for he always used his eyes, and very often—indeed rather oftener than was sometimes pleasant for the people about him if they wanted to be quiet—his tongue too, for he was great at asking questions.

"Soda's very useful," Ted reflected; "nurse says it makes things come cleaner."

Just then his mother called him.

"Ted, dear," she said, "I'm going."

Ted started and ran after her, but just as he did so, he stretched out his hand and took a lump of soda out of the barrel. He did it quite openly, he didn't mind in the very least if the shopman saw him—like the daisies in the field, so he thought, the soda and the sugar and the French plums and everything were there for him or for any one to help themselves to as they liked. But Ted was not greedy—he was far better pleased to get something "useful" for mother than anything for himself. He would have asked her what he had better take, if he had had time—he would have stopped to say "Thank you" to the grocer had he not been in such a hurry to run after his mother.

They walked quickly down the street. Ted's mother was a little absent-minded for the moment— she was thinking of what she had ordered, and hoping she had forgotten nothing. And holding her little boy by the one hand she did not notice the queer thing he was holding in the other. Suddenly she stopped before a boot and shoe shop.

"I must get baby a pair of shoes," she said. "She is such a little kicker, she has the toes of her cloth ones out in no time. We must get her a pair of leather ones I think, Ted."

"Ses, I sink so," said Ted.

So his mother went into the shop and asked the man to show her some little leather shoes. Ted looked on with great interest, but when the shoes were spread out on the counter and he saw that they were all *black*, he seemed rather disappointed.

"Muzzer," he said in a low voice, tugging at his mother's skirts, "I saw such bootly boo boots in the man's winder."

His mother smiled.

"Yes, dear," she replied, "they're very pretty, but they wouldn't last so long, and I suspect they cost much more."

Ted looked puzzled.

"What does thoo mean?" he said, but before his mother had time to explain, the active shopman had reached down the "bootly" boots and held them forward temptingly.

"They're certainly very pretty," said baby's mother,

who, to tell the truth, was nearly as much inclined for the blue boots as Ted himself. "What is the price of them?"

"Three and sixpence, ma'am," replied the man.

"And the black ones, the little black shoes, I mean?"

"Two and six," replied the man.

"A shilling difference, you see, Ted," said his mother. But Ted only looked puzzled, and his mother, occupied with the boots, did not particularly notice him.

"I think," she said at last, "I think I will take both. But as the blue boots will be best ones for a good while, give me them half a size larger than the little black shoes."

The shopman proceeded to wrap them up in paper and handed them to Ted's mother, who took out her purse and paid the money. The man thanked her, and, followed by her little boy, Ted's mother left the shop.

Ted walked on silently, a very unusual state of things. He was trying to find out how to express what he wanted to ask, and the ideas in his head were so new and strange that he could not fit them with words all at once. His mother turned round to him.

"Would you like to carry the parcel of baby's shoes for her?" she said.

"Oh ses," said Ted, holding out his left hand. But as his mother was giving him the parcel she noticed that his right hand was already engaged.

"Why, what have you got there?" she asked, "a stone? Where did you get it? No, it's not a stone —why, can it be a lump of soda?"

"Ses," returned Ted with the greatest composure, "it are a lump of soda. I thought it would be very suseful for thoo, so I took it out of that nice man's shop."

"My dear little boy!" exclaimed his mother, looking I don't know how. She was rather startled, but she could not help being amused too, only she thought it better not to show Ted that she was amused. "My dear little boy," she said again, "do you not understand? The things in the shop belong to the man— they are his, not ours."

"Ses," said Ted. "I know. But he lets thoo take them. Thoo took soap and somesing else, and he said he'd send them home for thoo."

"Yes, dear, so he did," said his mother. "But I *pay* him for them. You didn't see me paying him, because I don't pay him every time. He puts down all I get in a book, and then he counts up how much it is every month, and then I send him the money. In some shops I pay as soon as I get the things. You saw me pay the shoemaker for little Cissy's boots and shoes."

"Ses," said Ted, "I saw thoo take money out of thoo's purse, but I didn't understand. I thought all those kind men kept nice things for us to get whenever we wanted."

"But what did you think money was for, little Ted? You have often seen money, shillings and sixpences and pennies? What did you think was the use of it?"

"I thought," said Ted innocently, "I thought moneys was for giving to poor peoples."

His mother could hardly resist stooping down in the street to kiss him. But she knew it was better not. Ted must be made to understand that in his innocence he had done a wrong thing, and the lesson of to-day must be made a plain and lasting one.

"What would poor people do with money if they could get all the things they wanted out of the shops for nothing?" she said quietly.

Ted considered a moment. Then he looked up brightly.

"In course!" he said. "I never thought of that."

"And don't you see, dear Ted, that it would be wrong to take things out of a shop without paying for them? They *belong* to the man of the shop—it would be just like some one coming to our house and taking away your father's coat or my bonnet, or your little blue cart that you like so much, or——"

"Or Cissy's bootly boo boots," suggested Ted, clutching hold more tightly of the parcel, as if he thought the imaginary thief might be at hand.

"Yes," said his mother, "or Cissy's new boots, which are mine *now* because I paid money for them to the man."

"Ses," said Ted. Then a very thoughtful expression came into his face. "Muzzer," he said, "this soda was that man's—sall I take it back to him and tell him I didn't understand?"

"Yes," said his mother. "I do think it is the best thing to do. Shall we go at once? It is only just round the corner to his shop."

She said this thinking that little Ted would find it easier to do it at once, for she was sorry for her little boy having to explain to a stranger the queer mistake he had made, though she felt it was right that it should be done. "Shall we go at once?" she

I

repeated, looking rather anxiously at the small figure beside her.

"Ses," said Ted, and rather to her surprise his tone was quite bright and cheery. So they turned back and walked down the street till they came to the corner near which was the grocer's shop.

Ted's mother had taken the parcel of the little boots from him and held him by the hand, to give him courage as it were. But he marched on quite steadily without the least flinching or dragging back, and when they reached the shop it was he who went in first. He walked straight up to the counter and held out the lump of soda to the shopman.

"Please, man," he said, "I didn't know I should pay money for this. I didn't understand till muzzer told me, and so I've brought it back."

The grocer looked at him in surprise, but with a smile on his face, for he was a kind man, with little boys and girls of his own. But before he said anything, Ted's mother came forward to explain that it was almost the first time her little boy had been in a shop ; he had not before understood what buying and selling meant, but now that she had explained it to him, she thought it right for him himself to bring back the lump of soda.

"And indeed it was his own wish to do so," she added.

The grocer thanked her. It was not of the least consequence to him of course he said, but still he was a sensible man and he respected Ted's mother for what she had done. And then, half afraid that her little boy's self-control would not last much longer, she took him by the hand, and bidding the shopman good-day they left the shop. As they came out into the street again she looked down at Ted. To her surprise his little face was quite bright and happy.

"He were a kind man," said Ted; "he wasn't vexed with Ted. He knew I didn't understand."

"Yes, dear," said his mother, pleased to see the simple straightforward way in which Ted had taken the lesson; "but *now*, Ted, you do understand, and you would never again touch anything in a shop, would you?"

"Oh no, muzzer, in course not," said Ted, his face flushing a little. "Ted would *never* take nothing that wasn't his—*never*; thoo knows that, muzzer?" he added anxiously.

"Yes, my dear little boy," and this time his mother *did* stoop down and kiss him in the street.

CHAPTER VII.

GETTING BIG.

"The children think they'll climb a tree."

It was a very happy little Ted that trotted upstairs
to the nursery with the "bootly boo boots" and the
more modest little black shoes for tiny Narcissa.

"See what Ted has brought thoo," he said, kissing
his baby sister with the pretty tenderness he always
showed her, "and see what muzzer has gave *me*," he
went on, turning to nurse with another parcel.   In
his excitement he didn't know which to unfasten first,
and baby had got hold of one of the black shoes, fortunately not the blue ones, and was sucking it vigor-
ously before Ted and nurse saw what she was doing.

"*Isn't* she pleased?" said Ted, delightedly.   Baby
must be very pleased with her new possessions, to try
to *eat* them, he thought.   And then he had time to
examine and admire his own present.   It was a
delightful one—a book, a nice old-fashioned fat book

of all the old nursery rhymes, and filled with pictures
too. And Ted's pride was great when here and there
he could make out a word or two. Thanks to the
pictures, to his own good memory, and the patience
of all the big people about him, it was not long before
he could say nearly all of them. And so a new pleasure was added to these happy summer days, and to
many a winter evening to come.

That night when Ted was going to bed he said
his prayers as usual at his mother's knee.

"Make me a good little boy," he said, and then
when he had ended he jumped up for his good-night
kiss, with a beaming face.

"I sink God *has* made me good, muzzer?" he said.

"Do you, dear? I hope He is *making* you so," she
answered. "But what makes you say so?"

"'Cos I *feel* so happy and so good," said Ted, "and
thoo said I was good to-day when thoo kissed me.
And oh, *may* I take my sprendid hymn-book to bed
wif me?"

And with the ancient legends of Jack and Jill
and Little Boy Blue, and Margery Daw, safely under
his pillow, happy Ted fell asleep. I wonder if he
dreamt of them! What a pity that so much of the
pretty fancies and visions of little childhood are lost

to us! What quaint pictures they would make. What a heavy burden *should* lie on the consciences of those who, by careless words or unconsidered tone, destroy the lovely tenderness of little children's dreams and conceits, rub off the bloom of baby poetry!

I could tell you, dear little friends, many pretty stories of Ted and his tiny sister during the first sunny year of little Narcissa's life, but I daresay it may be more interesting to you to hear more of these children as they grow older. The day-by-day life of simple happy little people is, I trust, familiar to you all, and as I want you to *know* my boy Ted, to think of him through your own childhood as a friend and companion, I must not take up too much of the little book, so quickly filled, with the first years only of his life. And these had now come to an end—a change, to Ted a great and wonderful change, happened about this time. Before little Cissy had learnt to run alone, before Ted had mastered the longest words in his precious "hymn-book," these little people had to leave their beautiful mountain home. One day when the world was looking pensive and sad in its autumn dress, the good-byes had to be said—good-bye to the garden and Ted's shaky bridge; good-bye to old David; and alas! good-bye to Cheviott's grave, all that was left

of the faithful old collie to say good-bye to; good-bye
to the far-off murmur of the sea and the silent
mountain that little Ted had once been so afraid of;
good-bye to all of the dear old home, where Ted's
blue cart was left forgotten under a tree, where the
birds went on singing and chirping as if there were
no such things as good-byes in the world—and Ted
and Cissy were driven away to a new home, and the
oft-told stories of their first one were all that was left
of it to their childish minds.

A good many hours' journey from the mountains
and the sea near which these children had spent their
first happy years, in quite another corner of England,
there is to be found a beautiful, quiet old town. It is
beautiful from its position, for it stands on rising
ground; a fine old river flows round the feet of its
castle rock, and on the other side are to be seen high
cliffs with pleasant winding paths, sometimes descend-
ing close to the water's edge, and it is beautiful in
itself. For the castle is such a castle as is not to
be met with many times in one's life. It has taken
centuries of repose after the stormy scenes it lived
through in the long-ago days to make it what it now
is—a venerable old giant among its fellows, grim and
solemn yet with a dreamy peacefulness about it, that

has a wonderful charm. As you cross the unused
drawbridge and your footsteps sink in the mossy
grass of the great courtyard, it would not be difficult to fancy you were about to enter the castle
of the sleeping-beauty of the dear old fairy-tale
—so still and dream-like it seems, so strange it is to
picture to one's fancy the now grass-grown keep with
the din and clang of horsemen and men-at-arms that
it must once have known. And near by is a grand
old church, solemn and silent too, but differently so
from its twin-brother the castle. The one is like a
warrior resting after his battles, thinking sadly of the
wild scenes he has seen and taken part in; the other
like a holy man of old, silent and solemn too, but
with the weight of human sorrows and anxieties that
have been confided to him, yet ever ready to sympathise
and to point upwards with a hope that never fails.

These at least were the feelings that the sight of the
old church and the old castle gave *me*, children dear.
I don't suppose Ted thought of them in this way
when he first made their acquaintance, and yet I
don't know. He might not have been able to say
much of what he felt, he was such a little fellow. But
he *did* feel, and in a way that was strange and new,
and nearly took his breath away the first time he

entered the beautiful old church, walking quietly up
the aisle behind his father, his little hat in his hand,
gazing up with his earnest eyes at the mysterious
stretch of the lofty roof. "O mother," he said, when
he went home, "when I am big I will always like
the *high* church best." And when the clear ringing
chimes burst forth, as they did with ever-fresh beauty
four times a day, sounding to the baby fancy as if
they came straight down from heaven, it was all Ted
could do not to burst into tears, as he had done that
summer day when Mabel had sung "Home, sweet
home" in the mountain-gorge.

For it was in this old town, with its church and
castle and quaint streets, where some of the houses
are still painted black and white, and others lean forward in the top stories as if they wanted to kiss each
other; where the front doors mostly open right on to
the street, and you come upon the dear old gardens as
a sort of delicious surprise at the back; where each
turn as you walk about these same old streets gives
you a new peep, more delightful than the last, of the
river or the cliffs or the far distant hills with their
tender lights and shadows; where, on market days
the country people come trooping in with their poultry
and butter and eggs, with here and there a scarlet

cloak among them, the coming and going giving the old High Street the look almost of a foreign town;— here in this dear old place little Ted took root again, and learned to love his new home so much that he forgot to pine for the mountains and the sea. And, here, some years after we said good-bye to them as they drove away from the pretty house in the garden, we find them again—Ted, a big boy of nine or ten, Cissy looking perhaps older than she really was, so bright and hearty and capable a little maiden had she become.

They are in the garden, the dear garden that was as delightful a playing place as children could have, though quite, quite different from the first one you saw Ted in. There it was all ups and downs, lying as it did on the side of a hill; here the paths are on flat ground, though some are zigzaggy of course, as the little paths in an interesting garden always should be; while besides these, some fine broad ones run straight from one end to another, making splendid highroads for drives in wheelbarrows or 'toy-carts. And in this garden too the trees are high and well grown, and plenty of them. It was just the place for hide and seek or "I spy."

Ted and Cissy have been working at their gardens.

"Oh dear," said the little girl, throwing down her tiny rake and hoe, "Cissy *is* so tired. And the f'owers won't grow if they isn't planted kick. Cissy is so fond of f'owers."

"So am I," said Ted, "but girls are so quickly tired. It's no good their trying to garden."

Cissy looked rather disconsolate.

"Boys shouldn't have all the f'owers," she said. "Zoo's not a summer child, Ted, zoo's a Kismas child. Zoo should have snow, and Cissy should have f'owers."

She looked at her brother rather mischievously as she said this.

"As it happens, Miss Cissy," said Ted, "there wasn't any snow the Christmas I was born. Mother told me so. And any way, if you liked snowballs I'd let you have them, so I don't see why I shouldn't have flowers."

Cissy threw her arms round Ted's neck and kissed him. "Poor Ted," she said, "zoo shall have f'owers. But Cissy won't have any in her garden if zey isn't planted kick."

"Well, never mind. I'll help you," said Ted; "as soon as I've done my lessons this evening, I'll work in your garden."

"Zank zoo, *dear* Ted," said Cissy rapturously, and

a new hugging ensued, which Ted submitted to with a good grace, though lately it had dawned on him that he was getting rather too big for kissing.

The children's "gardens" were just under the wall that skirted their father's real garden. On the other side of this wall ran the highroad, and the lively sights and sounds to be heard and seen from the top of this same wall made the position of their own bit of ground greatly to their liking. Only the getting on to the wall! There was the difficulty. For Ted it was not so tremendous. *He* could clamber up by the help of niches which he had managed to make for his feet here and there between the stones, and the consequent destruction to trousers and stockings had never as yet occurred to his boyish mind. But Cissy —poor Cissy! it was quite impossible to get *her* up on to the wall, and for some time an ambitious project had been taking shape in Ted's brain.

"Cissy," he said, when he was released, "it's no good beginning working at your garden now. We have to go in in ten minutes. I'm going up on the wall for a few minutes. You stay there, and I'll call down to you all I see."

"O Ted," said Cissy, "I *wiss* I could climb up the wall too."

"I know you do," said Ted. "I've been thinking about that. Wait till I get up, and I'll tell you about it."

"Full of faith in Ted's wisdom, little Cissy sat down by the roots of a great elm-tree which stood in her brother's domain. "My tree" Ted had always called it, and it was one of the charms of his property. *It* was not difficult to climb, even Cissy could be hoisted some way up—to the level of top of the wall indeed, without difficulty, but unfortunately between the tree and the wall there was a space, too wide to cross. And even when the right level was reached, it was too far back to see on to the road.

"If only the tree grew close to the wall," Ted had often said to himself; and now as Cissy sat down below wondering what Ted was going to do, his quick eyes were examining all about to see if a plan that had struck him would be possible.

"Cissy," he cried suddenly, and Cissy started to her feet. "Oh what, Ted?" she cried.

"I see how it could be done. If I had a plank of wood I could fasten it to the tree on one side, and—and—I could find *some* way if I tried, of fastening it to the wall on the other, and then I could pull the branches down a little—they're nearly down far enough, to make a sort of back to the seat, and oh, Cissy, it would be such a lovely place! We could both sit on it, and see all that passed. I'll tell you what I'm seeing now. There's a man with a wheel-barrow just passing, and such a queer little dog run-ning beside, and farther off there's a boy with a basket, and two girls, and one of them's carrying a baby, and —yes there's a cart and horse coming—awfully fast. I do believe the horse is running away. No, he's pulled it up, and——"

"O Ted," said Cissy, clasping her hands, "how *lovely* it must be! O Ted, do come down and be kick about making the place for me, for Cissy."

Just then the dinner-bell rang. Ted began his descent, Cissy eagerly awaiting him. She took his hand and trotted along beside him.

"*Do* zoo think zoo can do it, Ted?" she said.

"I must see about the wood first," said Ted, not without a little importance in his tone; "I think there's some pieces in the coach-house that would do."

At luncheon the big people, of whom there were several, for some uncles and aunts had been staying with the children's father and mother lately, noticed that Ted and Cissy looked very eager about some-thing.

"What have you been doing with yourselves, you little people, this morning?" said one of the aunties kindly.

Cissy was about to answer, but a glance from Ted made her shut tight her little mouth again. There must be some reason for it—perhaps this delightful plan was to be a secret, for her faith in Ted was unbounded.

"We've been in the garden, in *our* gardens," Ted replied.

"Digging up the plants to see if they were growing—eh?" said an uncle who liked to tease a little sometimes.

Ted didn't mind teasing. He only laughed. Cissy looked a little, a very little offended. She did *not* like teasing, and she specially disliked any one teasing her dear Ted. Her face grew a little red.

"Ted knows about f'owers bootilly," she said; "Ted knows lots of things."

"*Cissy!*" said Ted, whose turn it was now to grow a little red, but Cissy maintained her ground.

"Ses," she said. "Ted does."

"Ted's to grow up a very clever man, isn't he, Cissy?" said her father encouragingly—"as clever as *Uncle* Ted here."

"Oh no," the little fellow replied, blushing still more, for Ted never put himself forward so as to be noticed; "I never could be that. Uncle Ted writes books with lots of counting and stick-sticks in them and——"

"Lots of *what?*" asked his uncle.

"Stick-sticks," said Ted simply. "I don't know what it means, but mother told me it was a sort of counting—like how many days in a year were fine and how many rainy."

"Or how many old women with baskets, and how many without, passed down the road this morning—eh, Ted?" said his other uncle, laughing heartily.

"Yes, I suppose so," said Ted. "Are stick-sticks any good?" he inquired, consideringly.

"It's to be hoped so," said Uncle Ted.

A bright idea struck the little fellow. He must talk it over with Cissy. If only that delightful seat between the tree and the wall was arranged *they* might make "stick-sticks"! What fun, and how pleased Uncle Ted would be! Already Ted's active brain began to plan it all. They should have a nice big ruled sheet of paper and divide it into rows, as for columns of sums: one row should be for horses alone, and one for horses with carts, and one for

people, and one for children, and another for dogs,
and another for wheelbarrows perhaps. And then
sometimes donkeys passed, and now and then pigs
even, on their way to market—yes, a lot of rows
would be needed. And at the top of the paper he
would write in nice big letters "stick"—no, mother
would tell him how to write it nicely, he knew that
wasn't quite the real word, mother would spell it for
him : "St—something—of what passed the tree." It
would be almost like writing a book.

He was so eager about it that he could hardly
finish his dinner. For a great deal was involved in
his plan, as you shall hear.

In the first place, it became evident to him after
an examination of the bits of wood in the unused
coach-house, that there was nothing there that would
do. He could get a nice little plank, a plank that
would not scratch poor Cissy's legs or tear her frocks,
from the carpenter, but then it would cost money, for
Ted had gained some worldly wisdom since the days
when he thought the kind shopkeepers spread out
their wares for everybody to help themselves as they
liked. And Ted was rather short of money, and Ted
was of rather an independent spirit. He would much
prefer not asking mother for any. The seat in the

K

tree would be twice as nice if he could manage it all his own self, as Cissy would say.

Ted thought it all over a great deal, and talked about it to Cissy. It was a good thing, they agreed, that it was holiday-time just now, even though Ted had every day *some* lessons to do. And though Cissy was very little, it was, after all, she who thought of a plan for gaining some money, as you shall hear.

Some few times in their lives Ted and Cissy had seen Punch and Judy, and most delightful they thought it. Perhaps I am wrong in saying Cissy had seen it more than once, but *Ted* had, and he used to amuse Cissy by acting it over to please her. And I think it was from this that her idea came.

" Appose, Ted," she said the next day when they were out in the garden having a great consultation— " appose we make a show, and all the big people would give us pennies."

Ted considered for a minute. They were standing, Cissy and he, by the railing which at one side of their father's pretty garden divided it from some lovely fields, where sheep, with their dear little lambs skipping about beside them, were feeding. Far in the distance rose the soft blue outlines of a lofty hill, " our precious hill " Ted's mother used to call it, and indeed it was almost worthy of the name of mountain, and for this she valued it still more, as it seemed to her like a reminder of the mountain home she had loved so dearly. Ted's glance fell on it, and it carried back his thoughts to the mountain of his babyhood and the ogre stories mixed up with it in his mind. And then his thoughts went wandering away to his old "hymn book," still in a place of honour in his bookshelves, and to the fairy stories at the end of it—Cinderella and the others. He turned to Cissy with a beaming face.

"I'll tell you what we'll do, Cis," he said; "we'll have a show of Beauty and the Beast. What a good idea it was of yours, Cis, to have a show."

Cissy was *greatly* flattered. Only she didn't quite like the idea of her dear Ted being the Beast. But when Ted reminded her that the Beast was *really* so good and kind, she grew satisfied.

"And how awfully pleased Percy will be when he comes to see the seat, *won't* he?" said Ted. And this thought reconciled him to what hitherto had been rather a grief to him—that Percy's holidays were shorter and fell later in the season than his.

You can imagine, children, better than I could tell what a bustle and fuss Ted and Cissy were in all

that day.   They looked so important, Ted's eyes were
so bright, and Cissy's little mouth shut close in such a
dignified way, that the big people must have been *very*
stupid big people not to suspect something out of the
common.   But as they were very kind big people, and
as they understood children and children's ways, they
took care not to seem as if they did notice, and
Mabel and her sister, who were also of the home party,
even helped Cissy to stitch up an old muslin window
curtain in a wonderful way for Beauty's dress, without
making any indiscreet remarks.   At which little Cissy
greatly rejoiced.   " *Wasn't* I clever not to let zoo find
out ?" she said afterwards, with immense satisfaction.

Late that evening—late for the children that is to
say—about seven o'clock, for Cissy had got leave to
sit up an hour longer, there came a ring at the hall
bell, and a very funny-looking letter was handed in,
which a boy in a muffled voice told the servant was
for the ladies and gentlemen, and that she was to tell
them the "act" would begin in five minutes "in the
theatre hall of the day nursery."   The parlour maid,
who (of course !) had not the least idea in the world
that the messenger was Master Ted, gravely handed
the letter to Miss Mabel, who was the first person she
saw, and Mabel hastened to explain to the others that

"Oh dear, oh dear!" cries Beauty, jumping up in a fright,
"he's coming to eat me."—P. 133.

its contents, quarters of old calling-cards with numbers marked on them, were evidently meant to be tickets for the performance. The big people were all much amused, but all of course were quite ready to "assist" at the "act." They thought it better to wait a little more than five minutes before going upstairs to the theatre hall, to give Ted time to get ready before the spectators arrived, not understanding, you see, that all he had to do was to pin his father's rough brown railway rug on, to imitate the Beast. So when they at last all marched upstairs the actors were both ready awaiting them.

There was a row of chairs arranged at one side of the nursery for the visitors, and the hearth-rug, pulled out of its place, with a couple of footstools at each side, served for the stage. Scene first was Miss Beauty sitting in a corner crying, after her father had left her in the Beast's garden.

"He'll eat me up! oh, he'll eat me up!" she sobs out; and then a low growl is heard, and from a corner behind a table where no one had noticed him, a very remarkable-looking shapeless sort of dark brown lump rolls or waddles along the floor.

"Oh dear, oh dear!" cries Beauty, jumping up in a fright, "he's coming to eat me."

"No, I'm not going to eat you, dear Beauty," the growly voice replies; "I'm not going to hurt you, dear Beauty. I've brought you something nice to eat for your tea. I'm sure you must be hungry;" and from somewhere or other the Beast produces a plate with some biscuits, which he humbly lays at her feet and then waddles off again. Beauty nibbles at the biscuits, then murmuring to herself, "He's a very kind Beast," she moves away, her window curtain train sweeping gracefully after her, behind the screen, which is supposed to represent the inside of the Beast's Castle, and where he himself has already disappeared. And this is the end of the first scene, the "act" being divided into two scenes.

The audience all clap their hands in applause.

"Capital!" and "Bravo!" they call out, so that Ted and Cissy feel their cheeks quite red, even behind the screen.

"Let's get it done quick, Cissy," said Ted; "it makes me feel so silly when they call out like that."

And the last scene is hurried on. It is not a very long one. Beauty has been away. She has gone, as everybody knows, on a visit to her old home, and on her return poor Beast is nowhere to be found. At last she discovers him lying quite still in a corner of the garden.

"Oh, poor Beast!" she exclaims, "Cis—Booty, I mean, is so sorry. Oh, poor Beast! I is afraid you is kite deaded, and I do love zoo, poor Beast," at which up jumps poor Beast, Beast no longer, for his rough skin rolls off as if by magic, and lo and behold there is Ted, got up ever so fine, with a scarlet scarf round his waist and an elegant old velvet smoking-cap with a long tassel on his head, and goodness knows what more.

"Oh, you bootiful P'ince," cries Beauty, and then they take hands and bow most politely to the audience, and then in a sudden fit of shamefacedness and shyness, they both scurry off behind the screen, Ted toppling over Cissy's long train on the way, at which there is renewed applause, and great laughter from the actors themselves. But the manager is quite up to his business. "That's all," calls out a little voice from behind the screen; "zoo may all go now, and *pay at the door.*" And sure enough as the big people make their way out, there is Ted in his usual attire standing at the door, with a little basket in his hand, gracefully held out for contributions.

"Why, how did you get here already?" asks his father.

"I slipped round by the other side of the screen while you were all laughing and clapping," says Ted, looking up with a beaming face. And the pennies and sixpennies that find their way into the basket are several. When the actors count up their gains before they go to bed, they are the happy possessors of two shillings and sevenpence. Far more than enough to pay for the wood for the seat in the tree!

CHAPTER VIII.

" STATISTICS."

" Are they not busy ?—the creatures !
Wanting to go to their beds ?—not they ! "

How delightful it was to wake the next morning and
to see sparkling in the early sunshine the neat little
silver coins, and the big copper ones, laid out in a row
on his table ! Ted jumped out of bed, not quite so
early as he had intended, for he had been up rather
later than usual the night before, and by the time he
had had his nice cold bath and was dressed, he heard
the prayer bell ring, and was only ready to take his
seat as usual on a little chair in a corner of the room
not far from where his dear old nurse and the other
servants were placed. He liked better to sit there,
for it gave him somehow a little uncomfortable feeling
to see the servants quite by themselves, as it were, so
separated from the family, and he had got into the way
of sitting between the two sets of seats, and though

little Narcissa from her perch on her mother's knee
would sometimes smile and nod and beckon to him
to come nearer, Ted always kept to his own place.
This morning many thoughts were dancing about his
brain, and it was a litttle difficult for him to listen
with his usual attention, even though it was one of
the chapters he was very fond of, especially when his
father read it in his nice clear voice.   It was that one
about the boy Jesus, staying behind His father and
mother to talk with the learned doctors in the temple,
and though some part of it puzzled Ted rather, yet he
liked to listen and think about it. How frightened that
father and mother must have been ! How was it that
Jesus knew that it was right for Him to stay behind
—even though it was without His father's and mother's
leave?   For other little boys it would have been
wrong, but then,—oh yes, of course, Jesus was not like
other little boys. If only they, if only he, Ted, could
learn to be more like *Him*, the one perfect Christmas
child ! And even the puzzling part of it grew clearer
as this unconscious prayer rose out of the innocent
heart.   For Ted's own father and mother, even if they
were frightened for a little, would not be *vexed* if he
did something without their leave that was good and
right.   Only it was difficult to tell, very difficult—

on the whole Ted felt that he understood what his
mother told him about being obedient, better than he
used. That was what God had given little boys fathers
and mothers for, for they, when they were good and
wise, could not but know best. When they were *not*
good and wise, like the fathers and mothers of some of
the poor London street boys he had heard of—oh, how
fearful that must be ! And then as his own father's
voice went on, it all came before Ted like a picture—
he had once seen a picture of it, he thought—the first
setting-out of old Joseph and the sweet-faced mother,
the distress and fear, the delight of finding the Child
again, and then the long walk home all together to
the carpenter's shop in the narrow Eastern street.
And, child-like, Ted's fancy turned again with the
association to what was before him this morning.
He was to go to the carpenter's to choose the wood
for the seat in the tree, and oh, how delightful it would
be to see it arranged, and how surprised Percy would
be, and what beautiful rows of stick-sticks Cissy and
he would be able to make to help Uncle Ted. All
kinds of pleasant hopes and fancies were racing round
Ted's brain again as he knelt down with the others to
listen to the prayer that followed the reading. It was
not till the murmured chorus of " Our Father," repeated

all together at the end, caught his ear, that with a sudden start Ted realised that he had not been listening.

He did feel sorry and ashamed, but he was so happy that morning, the world outside was so bright and sunny, and the people inside so kind and cheerful, as they all sat round the breakfast table, that Ted's self-reproach did not last. And as soon as he had finished the short morning lessons he had to do in the holidays, he got leave from mother to go off to order the plank for the seat.

It turned out a little dearer than he had expected. Two and sevenpence were the funds in hand.

"I could give you a piece of wood for much less of course, sir," said the good-natured carpenter, who was a great ally of Ted's, "but as you explain it to me it needs something more than a bit of wood, else it wouldn't be safe for you and the young lady to sit on;" and then he showed the boy how it should be done, with a small iron bolt driven into the wall and another of a different kind fixed to the tree. "Then," said he, "it will be as safe as safe, and I'll plane you a neat little seat with no splinters or sharp edges to tear Missy's frocks."

Ted was delighted. His quick eye caught at

once the carpenter's plan, and he saw how much more satisfactory and complete it would be than the rough idea he had had at first. But the price? Ted felt much afraid that here was to be the difficulty.

"How much will it cost, Mr. Newton?" he inquired anxiously.

The carpenter reflected a moment.

"Wood, so much; bolts, so much; nails; time;" Ted heard him half whispering to himself. Then he looked up.

"A matter of three shilling or so, sir," he replied. "I'll try that it shan't be more. But you see the bolts I have to buy, they're not things as we use every day. And for the time, sir, I'm not thinking much of that. The evenings are light now. I'll try and see to it myself after work's over."

"Thank you very much, Mr. Newton," said Ted. "I think it'll be all right. But I'd like first to tell my mother how much it will cost, and then I'll run back and settle about it."

"All right, sir," the carpenter replied; and after pausing a moment at the door to pat the great big gentle dog, that was lying there blinking in the sunshine, and thinking to himself that its eyes somehow reminded him of long ago Cheviott whom Ted still remembered, though Newton's dog wasn't at all the same kind, the boy ran off again, whistling as he went, with light dancing steps down the in-and-out zigzag streets of the old town, stopping a moment, eager as he was, to admire the peeps of lovely view he came upon now and then as he turned a corner, or crossed the open market-place.

He was in great spirits. Fivepence short he felt sure could easily be made up.

"Either mother will give it me," he thought, "or she'll find some way of my earning it. I'm sure she'd like it properly done, and there'll be no fear of Cissy or me hurting ourselves."

On he danced again, for now he was in more open ground, running along the country highroad where was his home. A few cottages stood not far from where he was passing—cottages of respectable people, with several of whom sociable Ted was on friendly terms, and just as he was nearing the first of these, a boy about his own age came out, a basket on his arm and in his hands something tied up in a cloth which he was carrying carefully. But boys will be boys!

"Good morning, Jamie," said Ted as they met,

for he recognised the boy as the son of a man living farther down the road, who had sometimes worked for his father; "where have you been, and what's that you've got?" and in pure fun Ted tapped with a switch he was carrying on the mysterious bundle.

Jamie looked up laughingly.

"O Master Ted," he was just beginning, but somehow—*how* I cannot tell, and I feel pretty sure that neither Ted nor Jamie could have told either—Ted's friendly tap had either distracted his attention so that he trod on a stone and lost his balance, or else it had destroyed the equilibrium of the bundle itself, so that almost before he had time even to say "O Master Ted," the mischief was done. Down plumped the bundle, with a crash of broken crockery, and a brown liquid at once oozed out through the cloth, making a melancholy puddle on the road. Jamie's half-spoken words changed into a cry of despair. It was the Sunday's dinner which had come to grief, the pie which his poor mother had prepared so carefully, and which he was taking home from his grandmother's, in whose oven it had been baking.

" Oh dear, oh dear, what ever *shall* I do?" cried

the poor little boy. What will mother say? Oh
dear, oh dear!—O Master Ted, what shall I do?"

Jamie's tears and sobs were pitiful. Ted, with
a pale concerned face stood beside him, speechless.

"It was all my fault, Jamie," he said at last.
"It's me your mother must scold, not you. I must
go home with you, and tell her it wasn't your fault."

"Oh but it were," sobbed the child. "Mother
always tells me to look neither to right nor to left
when I'm carrying anything like this here. Oh
deary me, what ever shall I do?"

He stooped down and untied the knots of the
large checked handkerchief in which the unfortunate
pie had been enveloped. The dish was all in pieces,
the gravy fast disappearing. Jamie gathered together, using the largest bit of the broken stoneware as a plate, some of the pieces of meat which
might still be eaten, and Ted, stooping down too,
helped him to the best of his ability. But it was
very little that could be saved from the shipwreck.
And then the two boys turned in the direction of
Jamie's home, Jamie sobbing all the way, and Ted
himself too appalled to know what to say to comfort
him.

Jamie's mother was a busy, hard-working woman.

She was kind to her children, but that is not to say that they never had a sharp word from her. And there were so many of them—more than enough to try the patience of a mother less worried by other cares. So poor Jamie had some reason to cry, and he did not attempt to prevent Ted's going home with him—alone he would hardly have dared to face the expected scolding.

She was at the door, or just inside it, as the boys made their appearance, with a big tub before her in which she was washing up some odds and ends, without which her numerous family could not have made their usual tidy appearance at church and Sunday school the next day. For it was Saturday, often a rather trying day to heads of households in every class. But Jim's mother was in pretty good spirits. She had got on with her work, Sunday's pie had been made early and sent on to granny's, and Jamie, who was a very careful messenger, would be back with it immediately, all ready to be eaten cold with hot potatoes the next day. So Sunday's dinner was off the good woman's mind, when suddenly a startling vision met her gaze. There was Jamie, red-eyed and tearful, coming down the road, and beside him the little Master from the Lawn House.

L

What could be the matter? Jamie had not hurt
himself, thus much was evident, but what was the
small and shapeless bundle he was carrying in the
handkerchief she had given him to cover the pie,
and what had come over the nice clean handkerchief
itself? The poor woman's heart gave a great throb
of vexation.

"What ever have ye done with the pie, Jamie?"
she exclaimed first in her anxiety, though she then
turned in haste to bid the little master "good
morning."

"O mother," Jamie began, his sobs bursting out
afresh, but Ted put him gently aside.

"Let me tell," he said. "I came on purpose.
If—if you please," he went on eagerly, though his fair
face flushed a little, "it was all my fault. I gave
Jim a little poke with my stick, quite in fun, and
somehow it made him drop the pie. But it isn't
his fault. You won't scold *him*, please, will you?"

Vexed as she was, Jamie's mother could not but
feel softened. Ted's friendly ways were well known
to his poorer neighbours, who with one voice pronounced him "a perfect little gentleman wherever
he goes."

"It's not much use scolding," she said gently

enough, but still with real distress in her tone which went to Ted's heart. "No use crying over spilt milk, as my master says. But still I do think Jamie might have been more careful. However, it can't be helped, but they'll have to do without a pie for dinner to-morrow. And thank you, Master Ted, for coming along of Jim for to tell me."

"But it wasn't Jim's fault. It was *all* mine," repeated Ted sadly. And then he bade the poor woman good-bye, and nodding to Jim, who was still wiping his eyes, though looking a good deal less frightened, the boy set off towards home again.

But how different everything looked—the sun was as bright, the air as pleasant as ten minutes before, but Ted's heart was heavy, and when at the garden gate he met his mother, who greeted him with her kind smile and asked him if he had settled with Newton about the seat, it was all poor Ted could do not to burst into tears. He was running past his mother into the house, with a hasty "Yes, thank you, mother, I'll tell you about it afterwards," for he had not yet made up his mind what he should say or do; it was his own fault, and he must suffer for it, that was his first idea, but his mother stopped him. The momentary glance at his face had been sufficient to show her that something was the matter.

"What is it, Ted, dear?" she said kindly and anxiously.

Ted's answer was a question, and a very queer question.

"Mother," he said, "how much do pies cost?"

"Pies," repeated his mother, "what kind of pies do you mean? Big ones, little ones, meat ones, or what?"

"Big ones, mother, at least *a* big one, and all made of meat, with crust at the top. And oh!" he exclaimed, "there was the dish! I daresay that cost a good deal," and his face grew sadder and sadder.

But his mother told him he really must explain, and so he did. "I didn't mean to tell you about it, mother," he said, "for it was my own fault, and telling you seems almost like asking for the money," and here poor Ted's face grew red again. "I thought the only thing to do was to take the *act* money, the two shillings and sevenpence, you know, mother, and give it to Jamie's mother, and just give up having the seat," and here Ted's repressed feelings were too much for him. He turned away his face and fairly burst into tears. Give up the seat!

Think of all that meant to him, poor boy. The pleasure for Cissy as well as his own, the delightful surprise to Percy, the rows of stick-sticks for his uncle. I don't think it was wonderful that Ted burst into tears.

"My poor boy," said his mother, and then she thought it over to herself for a little. She did not begin talking to Ted about how careless he had been, and that it must be a lesson to him, and so on, as many even very kind mothers are sometimes tempted to do, when, as *does* happen now and then in this rather contrary world, very small wrongdoings have very big results,—she could not feel that Ted had been much to blame, and she was quite sure it *would* be "a lesson to him," without her saying any more about it. So she just thought it over quietly, and then said,

"No, Ted. I don't quite think that would be right. Your giving up the seat would be punishing others as well as yourself—Cissy particularly—and that would not be right. I will see that Jamie and his brothers and sisters have something for their dinner to-morrow that will please them as much as the pie, and you must tell Newton to go on with the seat. and——"

"But, mother," interrupted Ted, "I won't be happy unless I pay it myself, the dinner I mean. It wouldn't be *fair*, if I didn't—would it, mother?" and he looked up with his honest, anxious blue eyes in his mother's face, so that she felt the same wish to stoop down and kiss him that had made her do so long ago in the street of the little country town near their old home.

"I was going on to speak about that," said his mother. "It will take all your money and a little more to pay Newton, you see, and you haven't any more."

"No, mother, but if I was to give up my library pennies?"—for Ted subscribed a penny a week to a children's library in the town, as he had long ago exhausted the home stores.

"That would take a *very* long time, and it would be a pity for you to lose your reading," said his mother. "But I'll tell you what—I will count the dinner as owing from you to me, and you will pay it as best you can, little by little. For every summer you get presents from your uncles or cousins when they are with us. I will count it two shillings and sixpence—the sixpence for the dish, and I know you will not forget to pay me."

"No indeed, mother, and thank you *so* much," said Ted, with a now really lightened heart. "Shall I tell Jamie about the dinner? I could go that way when I go back to Newton's. He will be so pleased. His mother didn't scold him, but yet I couldn't help being *very* sorry for him. His face did look so unhappy."

And when, after dinner, Ted ran off again, I think the pleasure of the good news in store for poor Jamie was quite as much in his mind as his own errand to Newton's.

The seat was a great success. Newton came that very evening to measure it exactly, and Ted had the satisfaction of making some suggestions which the carpenter thought very good ones, as to the best way of fastening it firmly. And on Monday evening the work was accomplished. Never, surely, were two birds in a nest more happy than Ted and Cissy, when, for the first time, they mounted up on to their airy throne. Their mother, busy among her flowers, was surprised by a sound of soft singing over her head, coming from at first she could not tell where. She stood still to listen—she had, for the moment, forgotten about the perch in the tree. But the words and the tune soon told her who it was. It was Ted at his old favourite, " Home, sweet home." Sweetly and softly his boyish voice rang out. The tears came into his mother's eyes, but she moved away silently. She did not want the children to know she was there. It seemed to take away the simplicity of his pretty singing for him to know that *any one*, even his mother, had been listening.

" He is very fond of music," she said to herself, " no doubt he has great taste for it," and the thought gave her pleasure. She pictured to herself happy future days when Ted and Cissy would be able to play and sing together—when as " big people," the brother and sister would continue the tender friendship that she liked so much to see.

Monday evening was too late to begin the important paper for Uncle Ted. But on Tuesday the children were up with the lark, armed with a long ruled sheet, divided by lines across the other way, into what Ted called several " compartments," a pencil or two, for though Cissy could not make figures, she could make little strokes, each of which stood for a one *something*. The words at the head of the " compartments " comprised everything which, with the slightest probability, *could* be expected to journey along the highroad.   Men, women, boys, girls, babies in perambulators, babies in nurses' arms; old women with baskets were considered a separate genus, and had a row to themselves ; carts with one horse, waggons with two, donkeys, dogs, pigs, cats, wheelbarrows.   And at one side Ted carefully marked the hour at which began and ended the " observations."   For, alas ! the children could not be *all* day at their post, though they did gravely purpose that they should take it in turn to go in to dinner, so that no passers-by should be unrecorded. But that mother could not agree to.   Dinner must be eaten, and with as much deliberation and propriety as usual, or else what was an interest and a pleasure would have to be discouraged.   And after all it was rather nice to have the paper exhibited and commented upon as they all sat round the luncheon-table, though Cissy looked as if she were not *quite* sure that she should not take offence for Ted, when one of the big people inquired why there wasn't a row for elephants and another for dancing-bears.

The long summer afternoon was spent in the same way.   Never surely had such a delightful occupation for two small people brimming over with life and energy, been discovered.   Two birds busied with arranging their nest could not have been more completely content.

"If this goes on," said the children's mother, laughing, when they did condescend to come in to tea, "I think we had better send a mattress and a pillow up to your seat, and let you stay there all night."

Ted and Cissy smiled, and in their hearts I rather think they were of opinion that what their mother proposed would be very nice. But, eager as they were, they were both very hungry, and it was evident that living in a tree did not destroy their appetite, for the quantity of slices of bread and butter which disappeared would have alarmed any one unaccustomed to the feats of little people in that way.

And tea over, off they set again. It was almost as if they were away on a visit somewhere, the house seemed so quiet, and the garden, so often at that time of day the scene of tremendous romps in which even nurse herself was coaxed to join, quite deserted. *Unless*—that is to say—you had passed under a certain tree and stood still to listen to the clatter going on overhead, though, thanks to the leafy branches, there was nothing to be *seen*.

" Can there be magpies up in that tree ?" would, I think, have been your first idea. And then, listening a little more attentively, you would have come to think that whether human or feathered they were very funny magpies indeed.

" Fifteen, *sixteen,* that makes. Hurrah, sixteen dogs since ten o'clock this morning. And, let's see, seven old women with baskets, and———"

" Them wasn't all *old,*" corrects the small voice of magpie number two ; " Jessie wif the eggs isn't old."

" Never mind ; if they've got baskets they *should* be old," replies Ted. " An old woman with a basket *sounds* right. Then there's five p'rambulators, oh, it *is* a long word to spell—it goes right out of its place into the other rows. I wish I'd just put ' babies in p'rams.' And then there's three pigs and horses, oh dear I can't count how many. It's getting too dark to see the strokes on the paper. I say, Cissy, just you get down and run in and ask for two or three dips. We can stick them up on the wall and have a beautiful lighting up, and then we can see everybody that passes."

Down clambered obedient Cissy—she was growing very alert by this time at making her way up and down—off she set to the house with her message.

" Dips, dips," she repeated to herself. " Ted says I'm to ask for two or three dips. I wonder what dips is."

She had not the slightest idea, but it never occurred to her to do otherwise than exactly what her brother had said. It was a funny little figure that presented itself to the children's mother, in the twilight, just as she was putting away her work and thinking it was really time for Ted and Cissy to come in, a shawl wrapped round and tied behind over her white pinafore, of which the part that could be seen was by no means as clean as it might have been, any more than the eager flushed little face, with its bright dark eyes and wavy hair tumbling over the forehead.

" My dear Cissy, what a *very* dirty little girl you are," said her mother, laughing. " You really look more like a gipsy than anything else."

" Does dipsies live up trees ?" inquired Cissy gravely. " Trees *is* rather dirty. But oh, mother, Ted wants me to ask you for two or three dips. *P'ease* give me zem."

" *Dips*," repeated her mother, " what in the world does he want dips for ?"

" Cissy doesn't know," replied the little girl.

" Cissy doesn't know what dips is. Cissy finks Ted said he would 'tick zem up on ze wall, to make it look pitty."

Her mother was very much amused.

" Dips are candles," she said. " I suppose Ted wants to light up the tree."

Her words made a light break over Cissy's face in the first place.

" Oh ses," said the little maiden, "it is getting so dark. Oh *do* give Ted some dips, *dear* mother —do, *do*."

But not any number of "do's" would have made mother agree to so dangerous a proceeding.

" My dear little girl, you would certainly set yourselves on fire, and the tree too," she replied. "But never mind," she went on, seeing the corners of Cissy's mouth going down with the thought of Ted's disappointment, "I will go out with you and explain to Ted."

Mother put a shawl over her shoulders and went out with her little girl. Some way off, Ted heard them coming.

" O Cis, have you got the dips ?" he cried. " I forgot to tell you to bring some matches too. I've had such hard work to see, and a lot of people

passed.   I *think* there was a woman and two boys.
I'll have to mark them down, when——"

"I've come with Cissy, Ted," replied his mother's
voice, to his surprise, "to tell you that it would
really be too much of a good thing to go on with
your observations all night.   And, in the first place,
you would certainly set yourself and Cissy and the
tree on fire, if I let you have candles up there.
Come down now, that's a good boy, and show me
your paper, and we'll pack it up to send to your
uncle by post."

"Very well, mother," said Ted, with his usual
cheery good-nature.   "I'm coming.   Here goes," and
in another minute he was beside her.   "You don't
know what a beautiful long paperful I've got.   I
don't want you to pack it up *yet*, mother.   Cissy
and I are going to keep it on ever so much longer,
aren't we, Cis ?"

And chattering merrily the children went in
with their mother.   But as she said to their father,
it really is to be doubted if they would not have
stayed in the tree all night, if Ted had got his wish
and arranged a "dip" illumination on the top of
the wall.

After all, that day in the tree was the last of

their "stick-sticks." The weather changed, and there was nearly a week of rain, and by the time it was over, children-like, Ted and Cissy had grown tired of the rows of strokes representing old women and donkeys and horses, and all the rest of them; the "observations" had lost their attraction for them. Still the pleasure was not quite over, for there was the packing of the big paper to send to Uncle Ted by post, and his letter of thanks in return. And Percy came home for the holidays, and greatly approved of the nest in the tree. And what the children did *not* do up there—what games they played, how they were by turns Robinson Crusoe hiding from the savages, King Charles in the oak at Boscobel, or, quainter still, how they all sometimes suddenly turned into squirrels and manufactured for themselves the most wonderful tails of old brush handles, and goodness only knows what, which stuck straight up behind and made the climbing to the nest by no means an easy matter—yes indeed, what they did *not* do up in the tree would be difficult to tell.

But it comes into my mind just now that I have never told you anything of Ted's indoor life. Hitherto it has seemed all summer days and gardens, has it not? And no doubt the boy's *greatest* happiness was in outdoor interests and employments. But of course it was not always summer and sunshine for Ted, any more than for any one else—and, Christmas child though he was, there were wintry days when even *he* had to stay in the house and find work and pleasures indoors. For winter does not mean nothing but bright frosty skies overhead, and crisp clean snow underfoot. There are dreary days of rain and mist and mud, when children are much better at home, and when mothers and nurses are more thankful than any one *not* a mother or nurse can imagine, to have to do with cheerful contented little people, who are "good at amusing themselves," and unselfish enough not to worry every one about them because it is a rainy day.

CHAPTER IX.

A PEACOCK'S FEATHER AND A KISS.

" We tried to quarrel yesterday.
    Ah ! . . . kiss the memory away."

IN Ted's pleasant home there was a queer little
room used for nothing in particular. It was a very
little room, hardly worthy indeed of the name, but
it had, like some small men who have very big
minds, a large window with a most charming view.
I think it was partly this which made Ted take
such a fancy to this queer little room in the first
place—he used to stand at the window when they
first came to the house and gaze out at the stretch
of sloping fields, with peeps here and there of the
blue river fringed with splendid trees, and farther off
still the distant hills fading away into the mysterious
cloudiness, the sight of which always gave him a
strange feeling as if he would like to cry—Ted
used to gaze out of this window for ever so long at
a time, till somehow the little room came to be

M

associated with him, and the rest of the family got
into the way of speaking of it as his. And gradually
an idea took shape in his mind which he consulted
his mother about, and which she was quite pleased
to agree to. Might he have this little room for his
museum? That was Ted's idea, and oh how eagerly
his blue eyes looked up into his mother's face for her
reply, and how the light danced in them with pleasure when she said " yes."

There were shelves in the little room—shelves
not too high up, some of them at least, for Ted to
arrange his curiosities on, without having to climb
on to a chair, and even Cissy, when she was trusted
as a great treat to dust some of the treasures, could
manage nicely with just a footstool. It would be
impossible to tell you half the pleasure Ted got out
of his museum. It was to him a sort of visible
history of his simple happy life, for nowhere did he
go without bringing back with him some curious stone
or shell, or bird's feather, or uncommon leaf even,
to be placed in his collection, both as a remem-
brance of his visit and as a thing of interest in itself.

There were specimens of cotton in its different
stages, of wool too, from a soft bit of fluff which
Ted had picked off a Welsh bramble, to a square

inch of an exquisitely knitted Shetland shawl, fine
as a cobweb, which Ted had begged from Mabel
when she was giving the remains of the shawl to
Cissy for her doll.   There were bits of different
kinds of coal; there was "Blue John" from a Derby-
shire cavern, and a tiny china doll which, much
charred and disfigured, had yet survived the great
fire of Chicago, where one of the children's uncles
had passed by not long after; there was a bit of
black bread from the siege of Paris; there were all
manner of things, all ticketed and numbered, and
their description neatly entered in a catalogue which
lay on a little table by the door, on which was also
to be seen another book, in which Ted requested
all visitors to the museum to write their names, and
all the big people of the family so well understood
the boy's pride and pleasure in his museum, that no
one ever thought of making his way into his little
room without his invitation.

Ted had begun his museum some months before
the great excitement of the nest in the tree, but the
delights of the long summer days out of doors had
a little put it out of his head.   But the latter part,
as well as the beginning of these holidays, happened
to be very rainy, and the last fortnight was spent

mostly by Percy and Ted in the tiny museum room, where Percy helped Ted to finish the ticketing and numbering that he had not long before begun. And Cissy, of course, was as busy as anybody, flopping about with an old pocket-handkerchief which she called her duster, and reproving the boys with great dignity for unsettling any of the trays she had made so " bootily clean."

" You must try to get some more feathers, Ted," said Percy. " They make such a pretty collection. There's a fellow at our school that has an awful lot. He fastens them on to cards—he's got a bird-of-Paradise plume, an awful beauty. Indeed he's got two, for he offered to sell me one for half-a-crown. Wouldn't you like it ?"

" I should think I would," said Ted, " but I can't buy anything this half. You know my money's owing to mother for that that I told you about."

He gave a little sigh ; the bird of Paradise was a tempting idea.

"*Poor* Ted," said Cissy, clambering down from her stool to give him a hug.

Ted accepted the hug, but not the pity.

" No, Cissy. I'm not poor Ted for that," he said merrily. " It was ever so kind of mother to put it

all right, and ever so much kinder of her to do it
that way. I shouldn't have liked not to pay it
myself."

" I'll see if I can't get that fellow to swop his
bird of Paradise for some of my stamps, when I go
back to school," said Percy.

" Oh, thank you, Percy," said Ted, his eyes
shining.

" Anyway you might have some peacocks'," Percy
went on. " They're not so hard to get, and they
look so pretty."

" Mother's got some screens made of them on the
drawing-room mantelpiece," said Ted, " and one of
them's got a lot of loose feathers sticking out at the
back that are no use. Perhaps she'd give me one
or two. Then I could make a nice cardful, with
the peacocks' at the corners and the little ones in a
sort of a wreath in the middle."

He looked at the sheet of white paper on to
which, at present, his feathers were fastened. " Yes,
it would be very pretty," he repeated. But just
then the tea-bell rang, and the children left the
museum for that day.

The boys were in it the next morning, when Ted's
mother appeared with a rather graver face than

usual. She did not come in, she knew that Ted was putting all in perfect order, and that he did not want her to see it till complete, so she only slightly opened the door and called him out.

"Ted," she said quietly, but Ted saw that she was sorry, "Ted, do you know anything of this?"

She held up as she spoke a pretty and valuable little china ornament which always stood on the drawing-room mantelpiece. It was broken—quite spoilt—it could never be the same again.

"Oh dear," exclaimed Ted, "what a pity! Your dear little flower-basket. I am so sorry. How could it have got broken?"

"I don't know," said his mother. "I found it lying on the floor. It seemed as if some one had knocked it over without knowing. You are sure you were not trying to reach anything off the mantelpiece yesterday evening?"

"Sure," said Ted, looking sorry and puzzled.

"It stood just in front of my screen of peacock feathers," his mother went on. She did not in the very very least doubt his assurance, but his manner gave her the feeling that if she helped his memory a little, he might be able to throw some light on the mystery.

"In front of the peacock-feather fan," he repeated absently.

"Yes," said his mother, "but do not say anything about it, Ted. We may find out how it happened, but I do not like questioning every one about it. It gives the servants a feeling that I don't trust them, for they always tell me if they break anything. So don't say anything more about it to *any one.*"

"No," said Ted. His tone and manner were still a little puzzled, as if something was in his mind which he could not make clear to himself, and his mother, knowing that he sometimes was inclined to take things of the kind too much to heart, made up her mind to think no more about her poor little vase, and to treat its breakage as one of the accidents we have all to learn to bear philosophically in daily life. But though no more was said, Ted did not forget about it: it worried and puzzled him behind other thoughts, as it were, all day, and little did he or his mother think who was really the innocent culprit.

Late that night, just before going to bed herself, Ted's mother glanced into his room, as she often did, to see that the boy was sleeping peacefully. The light that she carried she shaded carefully, but a very wide-awake voice greeted her at once.

"Mother," it said, "I'm not asleep. Mother, I do so want to speak to you. I've not been able to go to sleep for thinking about the little broken vase."

"O Ted, dear," said his mother, "don't mind about it. It is no use vexing oneself so much about things when they are done and can't be put right."

"But, mother," he persisted, "it isn't quite that. Of course I'm *very* sorry for it to be broken, however it happened. But what makes me so uncomfortable is that I've begun to wonder so if perhaps I *did* do it. I know we were all talking about your peacock-feather screens yesterday. I said to Percy and Cissy there were some loose ones in one of them, and perhaps you'd give me some for my card of feathers, and I've got a sort of wondering feeling whether perhaps I *did* touch the screen and knocked down the china flower-basket without knowing, and it's making me so unhappy, but I *didn't* mean to hide it from you if I did do it."

He looked up so wistfully that his mother's heart felt quite sore. She considered a minute before she replied, for she was afraid of seeming to make light of his trouble or of checking his perfect honesty, and yet, on the other hand, she was wise, and knew that even conscientiousness may be exaggerated and grow into a weakness, trying to others as well as hurtful to oneself.

"I am sure you did not mean to hide anything from me, dear Ted," she replied, "and I don't think it is the least likely that you did break the vase. But even if you did, it is better to think no more about it. You answered me sincerely at the time, and that was all you could do. We are only human beings, you know, dear Ted, always likely to make mistakes, even to say what is not true at the very moment we are most anxious to be truthful. We can only do our best, and ask God to help us. So don't trouble any more, even if we never find out how it happened."

Then she stooped and gave Ted an extra good-night kiss, and in five minutes his loving anxious little spirit was asleep.

But the very next day the mystery was explained.

"Ted's *new*seum is bootly neat," Cissy announced at breakfast-time, "but he wants some more fevvers. I tried to get down muzzer's screen off the mantel-piece to see if there was some loose ones, but I couldn't reach it. Muzzer, *won't* you give Ted some loose ones ?"

Mother looked at Ted, and Ted looked at mother.

"So *you* were the mouse that knocked over my little vase, Miss Cissy!" said mother. "Do you know, dear, that it was broken? You should not try to reach things down yourself. You will be having an accident, like 'Darling' in the picture-book, some day, if you don't take care."

The corners of Cissy's mouth went down, and her eyes filled with tears.

"I didn't know," she said in a very melancholy voice. "I only wanted to find some loose fevvers for Ted.'"

"I know that, dear," said her mother. "Only if you had asked me you would have got the feathers without breaking my vase. Come with me now, and you'll show me what you want."

There proved to be two or three loose feathers as Ted had said—beautiful rainbow eyes, which would not be missed from the screen with the careful way in which Ted's mother cut them out, and the children carried them off in delight. They were neatly tacked on to the feather card, which had a very fine effect on the wall of the museum. And for both Ted and Cissy there was a little lesson, though the two were of different kinds, fastened up with the feathers on the card.

"They were neatly tacked on to the feather card, which had a very
fine effect on the wall of the museum."—P. 170.

Before long the holidays were over. Percy went back to school, and poor Ted hid himself for a few hours, as he always did on these sad occasions, that his red eyes might not be seen. Then he came out again, looking paler than usual, but quite cheerful and bright. Still he missed Percy so much that he was not at all sorry that his own holidays were over. For Ted now went early every morning to a regular big school—a school at which there were so many boys that some little fellows of his age might have felt frightened and depressed. But not so Ted. He went on his own cheery way without misgiving. The world to his thinking was a nice and happy place—not *all* sunshine of course, but very good of its kind. And school-life, though it too had its shadows, was full of interest and satisfaction. Ted loved his fellows, and never doubted, in his simple taking-for-granted of things being as they should be, but that he was loved by them; and how this way of looking out on the world helped him through its difficulties, how it saved him from unreasonable fears and exaggerated anxieties such as take the bloom off many a child-life, it would be difficult for me to describe. I can only try to put you in the way of imagining this bright young life for yourselves.

The boy whom, of course only *next* to his dear
Percy, Ted loved best in the world was, to use his
own words, "a fellow" of about his own age, whose
name was Rex.   That is to say, his short name;
for his real one was Reginald, just as Ted's was
Edmond.   They had been together at the big school
from the first of Ted's going, being about equal in
their standing as to classes, though Rex was rather
the elder, and had been longer at school.   At Ted's
school, as at all others, there were quarrels and fights
sometimes; and many a day he came home with
traces of war, in the shapes of bumps and bruises
and scratches.   Not that the battles were all *quarrels,* — there were plenty of good-tempered scrim-
mages, as well as, occasionally, more serious affrays,
for boys will be boys all the world over.   And,
worse than that, in all schools there are to be found
boys of mean and tyrannical spirit, who love to
bully and tease, and who need to be put down now
and then.   And in all schools, too, there are boys
of good and kindly feelings, but of hasty and un-
controlled temper, and they too have to be taught
to give and take, to bear and forbear.   And then,
too, as the best of boys are *but* boys after all, we
are still a long way off having any reason to ex-

pect that the best of schools even can be like dove-cots.

I don't know that Ted's school was worse than others in these respects, and Ted himself was not of a quarrelsome nature, but still in some ways he was not very patient. And then, slight and rather delicate though he was, he assuredly had a spirit of his own. He couldn't stand bullying, either of himself or others, and without any calculation as to the odds for or against him, he would plunge himself into the thick of the fray; and but for Rex, who was always ready to back up Ted, I daresay he would often have come off worse than he did. As it was, many were the wounds that fell to his share, and yet he managed, by his quickness and nimble-ness, to escape more serious damage.

"What have you been doing with yourself, my boy?" his mother said one day not long after the grand doing-up of the museum, when Ted appeared in her room on his return from school, to beg for some sticking-plaister and arnica lotion. He really looked rather an object, and he could not help laughing as he caught sight of his face in the glass; for one eye was very much swollen, and a long scratch down his nose did not add to his beauty.

"I *am* a fright," he said. "But there's not much the matter, mother. It was only a scrimmage —we were all quite good friends."

"But really, Ted," said his mother, "I think you must curb your warlike tastes a little. Some day you may really get hurt badly."

"No fear, mother," he said. "Besides, after all, a boy wouldn't be worth much who couldn't fight sometimes, would he ? "

"*Sometimes*," said his mother. "Where was Rex to-day—wasn't he beside you ? "

Ted's face clouded a little.

"Rex was in a bad humour to-day. He wouldn't play," Ted replied.

"Rex in a bad humour!" repeated his mother. "Surely that's very uncommon."

Ted did not reply, and his mother did not ask him any more, but she noticed that the cloud had not entirely disappeared, and the next morning it was not quite with his usual springing steps that the boy set off to school. Rex's house was on the same road; most days the boys met each other at the gate and went on together, but this time no Rex was to be seen. Either he had taken it into his head to go very early, or he was not yet ready.

Ted cast a glance towards the path, down which he was used to see his friend running, satchel over his shoulders, to join him—then he walked on slowly.

"I'm not going to wait for him if he doesn't care to come," he said to himself; and when he got to school he was glad he had not done so, for there was Rex already in the schoolroom, and at his desk busy writing, though it wanted some minutes to school-time.

"Good morning, Rex," said Ted.

"Good morning," replied Rex; but that was all. Whether or not he had been in a bad humour the day before, he was certainly not in a pleasant frame of mind towards Ted *to-day*. The morning passed much less cheerfully than usual, for when all was happy between the boys, though they could not speak to each other in school hours, there were many pleasant little ways in which they could make each other feel that his friend was next door. Ted's lessons suffered from his preoccupation, and, altogether, things seemed to go the wrong way. But Ted did not seem able to care. "What was the matter with Rex?" That was the one question always in his mind.

School over, the boys could not help meeting.

Their roads lay together, and both had too much self-respect to wish to make an exhibition of the want of good feeling between them to the other boys. So they set off as if nothing were the matter, and walked some little way in silence. At last Ted could stand it no longer.

"What's the matter with you, old fellow?" he said. "Why wouldn't you play with me yesterday?"

Rex looked up.

"I couldn't," he said. "I had got my French exercise all blotted, and I wanted to copy it over without telling any one; that was why I wouldn't come out. So *now* you see if it was true what you said of me to Hatchard."

"What did I say of you to Hatchard?" cried Ted.

"*What?* Why, what he told me you said— that I was a mean sneak, and that I wouldn't play because I wasn't as good at it as you."

"I never said so, and you know I never did," retorted Ted, his cheeks flaming.

"Do you mean to say that I'm telling a lie?" cried Rex in his turn.

"Yes I do, if you said I said that," exclaimed Ted. And then—how it happened I don't think

either of the boys could have told—their anger grew
from words into deeds.   Rex hit Ted, and Ted hit
at him again !   But one blow—one on each side—
and they came to their senses.   Ted first, when he
saw the ugly mark his clenched fist had left on his
friend's face, when he felt the hot glow on his
own.

"O Rex," he cried, "O Rex !   How can we be
like that to each other ?   It's like Cain and Abel.
O Rex, I'm so sorry !"

And Rex was quick to follow.

"O Ted, I didn't mean it.   Let's forget we ever.
did it.   I *do* believe you never said that.   Hatchard's
a mean sneak himself.   I only didn't want to tell
you that it was you who blotted my exercise by
mistake when you passed my desk.   I thought you'd
be so sorry.   But it would have been better to tell
you than to go on like this."

Rex's explanation was too much for Ted.   Ten
years old though he was, the tears rushed to his eyes,
and he felt as if he could never forgive himself.

He told his mother all about it that evening.
He could not feel happy till he did so, and even
before he had said anything she knew that the little
tug to her sleeve and the whispered "Mother, I want

N

to speak to you," was coming. And even when he had told her all about the quarrel and reconciliation, he hung on, looking as if there were something more to tell.

"What is it, my boy?" said his mother; "have you anything more to say?"

Ted's face flushed.

"Yes, mother," he said. "I wanted to ask you this. When Rex and I had settled it all right again, we still felt rather unhappy. It did seem so horrid to have hit each other like that, it seemed to leave a mark. So, mother, we wanted to take it quite away, and we *kissed* each other. And we felt quite happy, only—was it a very babyish thing to do? Was it *unmanly*, mother?"

His mother drew him towards her and looked lovingly into his anxious face.

"Unmanly, my boy? No indeed," she said, "it was kind and good, and kindness and goodness can never be unmanly."

And Ted, quite at rest now, went off to bed.

CHAPTER X.

SOME RAINY ADVENTURES.

" Wildly the winds of heaven began to blow,

   .   .   .   .   .   .

Whilst from the jealous, unrelenting skies
The inevitable July down-pour came."

ANOTHER winter came and went. Ted had another
birthday, which made him eleven years old. Another happy Christmas time—this year of the old-
fashioned snowy kind, for even in November there
was skating, and Ted skated like a Dutchman; and
the child - life in the pleasant home went on its
peaceful way, with much of sunshine and but few
clouds. Narcissa, too, was growing a big girl. She
could say all her words clearly now, without lisping
or funny mistakes, though, as she was the youngest
bird in the nest, I am not sure but that some of the
big people thought this rather a pity! And then
when the frost and the snow were done with, the ever
new spring time came round again, gradually growing into the brilliant summer; and this year the

children's hearts rejoiced even more than usual, for a great pleasure was before them. This year they were to spend the holidays with their parents in a quite, *quite* country place, and many were the delightful fancies and dreams that they made about it, even while it was some distance off.

"I do love summer," said Cissy one day. They were standing at the window one May morning, waiting for their father and mother to come to breakfast. It was a Sunday morning, so there was no hurrying off to school. "Don't you *love* summer, Ted ?"

"Yes, summer's awfully jolly," he replied. "But so 's winter. Just think of the snowballing and the skating. I do hope next winter will be a regular good one, for I shall· be ever so much bigger I expect, and I'll try my best to beat them all at skating."

His face and eyes beamed with pleasure. Just then his mother came in; she had heard his last words.

"Next winter !" she said. "That's a long time off. Who knows what may happen before then ?"

She gave a little sigh; Ted and Cissy looked at each other. They knew what mother was thinking of. Since *last* winter a great grief had come to her. She had lost one who had been to her what Ted was to Cissy, and the sorrow was still fresh. Ted and Cissy drew near to their mother. Ted stroked her hand, and Cissy held up her rosy mouth for a kiss.

"Dear mother," they said both together, and then a little silence fell over them all. Cissy's thoughts were sad as she looked at Ted and pictured to herself how terrible it would be to lose a brother as dear as he, and Ted was gazing up at the blue sky and *wondering*—wondering about the great mystery which had lately, for the first time in his life, seemed to come near him. What *was* dying? Why, if it meant, as his father and mother told him, a better, and fuller, and nobler life than this, which he found so good and happy a thing, why, if it meant living nearer to God, understanding Him better, why should people dread it so, why speak of it as so sad?

"I don't think," thought little Ted to himself, "I don't *think* I should be afraid of dying. God is so kind, I couldn't fancy being afraid of Him; and heaven must be so beautiful," for the sunny brightness of the May morning seemed to surround everything. But his glance fell on his mother and sister, and other thoughts rose in his mind; the leaving them—ah yes, *that* was what made death so sad a thing; and he had to turn his head away to hide the tears which rose to his eyes.

There was, as his mother had said, a long time to next winter—there seemed even, to the children, a long time to next summer, which they were hoping for so eagerly. And an interruption came to Ted's school-work, for quite unexpectedly he and Cissy went away to London for a few weeks with their parents, and when they came back there was only a short time to wait for the holidays. If I had space I would like to tell you about this visit to London, and some of the interesting things that happened there—how the children had rather a distressing adventure the first evening of their arrival, for their father and mother had to go off with their aunt in a hurry to see a sick friend, and, quite by mistake, their nurse, not knowing the children would be alone, went out with a message about a missing parcel, and poor Cissy, tired with the journey and frightened by the dark, rather gloomy house and the strange servants, had a terrible fit of crying, and clung to Ted as her only protector in a manner piteous to see. And Ted soothed and comforted her as no one else could have done. It was a pretty sight (though it grieved their mother too, to find that poor Cissy had been frightened) to see the little girl in Ted's arms, where she had fallen asleep, the tears still undried on her cheeks; and the next morning, when she woke up fresh and bright as usual, she told her mother that Ted had been, oh so kind, she never could be frightened again if Ted was there.

There were many things to surprise and interest the children, Ted especially, in the great world of London, of which now he had this little peep. But as I have promised to tell you about the summer I must not linger.

When they went back from town there were still eight or nine weeks to pass before the holidays, and Ted worked hard, really very hard, at school to gain the prize he had been almost sure of before the interruption of going away. He did not say much about it, but his heart *did* beat a good deal faster than usual when at last the examinations were over and the prize-giving day came round; and when all the successful names were read out and his was not among them, I could not take upon myself to say that there was not a tear to wink away, even though there was the consolation of hearing that he stood second-best in his class. And

Ted's good feeling and common sense made him look quite bright and cheerful when his mother met him with rather an anxious face.

"You're not disappointed I hope, Ted, dear, are you?" she said. "You have not taken quite as good a place as usual, and I did think you might have had a prize. But you know I am quite pleased, and so is your father, for we are satisfied you have done your best, so you must not be disappointed."

"I'm not, mother," said Ted cheerily,—"I'm not really, for you know I am *second*, and that's not bad, is it? Considering I was away and all that."

And his mother felt pleased at the boy's good sense and fair judgment of himself—for there had sometimes seemed a danger of Ted's entire want of vanity making him too timid about himself.

What a happy day it was for Ted and Cissy when the real packing began for the summer expedition! It's an ill wind that blows nobody any good, and I suppose it is by this old saying explained how it is that packing, the horror of mothers and aunts and big sisters, not to speak of nurses and maids, should be to all small people the source of such delight.

"See, Ted," said Cissy, "do let's carry down

some of these boxes. There's the one with the sheets and towels in, *quite* ready," and the children's mother coming along the passage and finding them both tugging with all their might at really a very heavy trunk, was reminded of the day—long ago now—in the mountain home, when, setting off for the picnic, wee Ted wanted so much to load himself with the heaviest basket of all !

And at last, thanks no doubt to these energetic efforts in great part, the packing was all done ; the last evening, then the last night came, and the excited children went to sleep to wake ever so much earlier than usual to the delights of thinking *the* day had come !

It was a, long and rather tiring railway journey, and when it came to an end there was a very long drive in an open carriage, and by degrees all houses and what Ted's father called " traces of civilisation," —which puzzled Cissy a good deal—were left behind.

" We must be getting close to the moors," said he, at which the children were delighted, for it was on the edge of these great moors that stood the lonely farm-house that was to be their home for some months. But just as their father said this, the carriage stopped, and they were told they must all get down—they were at the entrance to a wood through which there was no cart or carriage road, only a footpath, and the farm-house stood in a glen some little way on the other side of this wood. It was nearly dark outside the wood, inside it was of course still more so, so dark indeed that it took some care and management to find one's way at all. The children walked on quietly, Ted really enjoying the queerness and the mystery of this adventure, but little Narcissa, though she said nothing, pressed closer to her mother, feeling rather " eerie," and some weeks after she said one day, " I don't want ever to go home again because of passing through that dark wood."

But once arrived, the pleasant look of everything at the farm-house, and the hearty welcome they received from their host and hostess, the farmer and his wife, made every one feel it had all been worth the journey and the trouble. And the next morning, when the children woke to a sunny summer day in the quaint old house, and looked out on all sides on the lovely meadows and leafy trees, with here and there a peep of the gleaming river a little farther down the glen, and when, near at hand, they heard the clucking of the hens and the mooing of the

calves and the barking of the dogs, and all the delightful sounds of real farm-life, I think, children,
you will not need me to try to tell you how happy
our children felt. The next few days were a sort
of bewilderment of interests and pleasures and sur-
prises—everything was so nice and new—even the
funny old-fashioned stoneware plates and dishes
seemed to Ted and Cissy to make the dinners and
teas taste better than anything they had ever eaten
before. And very soon they were as much at home
in and about the farm-house as if they had lived
there all their lives,—feeding the calves and pigs,
hunting for eggs, carrying in wood for Mrs. Crosby
to help her little niece Polly, a small person not
much older than Cissy, but already very useful in
house and farm work. One day, when they were busy
at this wood-carrying, a brilliant idea struck them.

"Wouldn't it be fun," said Ted, "to go to the
wood—just the beginning of it, you know—and
gather a lot of these nice little dry branches; they
are so beautiful for lighting fires with?"

Cissy agreed that it would be great fun, and
Polly, who was with them at the time, thought, too,
that it would be very nice indeed; and then a still
better idea struck Ted. "Suppose," he said, "that

we were to go to-morrow morning, and take our luncheon with us. Wouldn't *that* be nice? We could pack it in a basket and take it on the little truck that we get the wood in, and then we could bring back the little truck full of the dry branches."

The proposal was thought charming, and mother was consulted; and the next morning Mrs. Crosby was busy betimes, hunting up what she could give to her "honeys" for their picnic, and soon the three set off, pulling the truck behind them, and on the truck a basket carefully packed with a large bottle of fresh milk, a good provision of bread and butter, a fine cut of home-made cake, and three splendid apple turnovers. Could anything be nicer? The sun was shining, as it was right he should shine on so happy a little party, as they made their way up the sloping field, through a little white gate opening on to a narrow path skirting the foot of the hill, where the bracken grew in wild luxuriance, and the tall trees overhead made a pleasant shade down to the little beck, whose chatter could be faintly heard. And so peaceful and sheltered was the place, that, as the children passed along, bright-eyed rabbits stopped to peep at them ere they scudded away, and the birds hopped fearlessly across the path,

nay, the squirrels even, sitting comfortably among
the branches, glanced down at the three little figures
without disturbing themselves, and an old owl blinked
at them patronisingly from his hole in an ancient
tree-trunk. And by and by as the path grew more
rugged, Polly was deputed to carry the basket, for
fear of accidents, for Cissy pulling in front and Ted
pushing and guiding behind, found it as much as
they could do to get the truck along. How they
meant to bring it back when loaded with branches I
don't know, and as things turned out, the question did
not arise. The truck and the basket and the children
reached their destination safely; they chose a nice
little grassy corner under a tree very near the entrance
to the big wood, and after a *very* short interval of rest
from the fatigues of their journey, it was suggested
by one and agreed to by all that even if it were
rather too early for real luncheon or dinner time,
there was no reason why, if they felt hungry, they
should not unpack the basket and eat! No sooner
said than done.

"We shall work at gathering wood all the better
after we've had some refreshment," observed Ted
sagely, and the little girls were quite of his opinion.
And the rabbits and the owls and the squirrels must,

I think, have been much amused at the quaint little party, the spice cake and apple-turnover collation that took place under the old tree, and at the merry words and ringing laughter that echoed through the forest.

An hour or so later, the children's mother, with an after-thought of possible risk to them from the damp ground, made her way along the path and soon discovered the little group.   She had brought with her a large waterproof cloak big enough for them all to sit on together, but it was too late, for the refection was over ; the basket, containing only the three plates and the three tin mugs, propped up between Ted and Cissy, toppled over with the start the children gave at the sound of their mother's voice, and a regular " Jack and Jill " clatter down the slope was the result.   The children screamed with delight and excitement as they raced after the truant mugs and plates, and their mother, thinking that her staying longer might cause a little constraint in the merriment, turned to go, just saying cheerfully, " Children, I have brought my big waterproof cloak for you to sit on, but as your feast is over I suppose you won't need it.   What are you going to do next ?"

" O mother, we're just going to set to work," Ted's voice replied ; " we're having such fun."

" Well, good-bye then. I am going a walk with your father, but in case of a change of weather, though it certainly doesn't look like it, I'll leave the cloak."

She turned and left them. An hour or two later, when she came home to the farm-house and stood for a moment looking up at the sky, it seemed to her as if her remark about the weather had been a shadow of coming events. For the bright blue sky had clouded over, a slight chilly breeze ruffled the leaves as if in friendly warning to the birds and the butterflies to get under shelter, and before many moments had passed large heavy drops began to fall, which soon grew into a regular downpour. What a changed world !

" What will the children do ?" was the mother's first thought as she watched it. " It is too heavy to last, and fortunately there is no sign of thunder about. I don't see that there is anything to be done but to wait a little ; they are certain to be under shelter in the wood, and any one going for them would be drenched in two minutes."

So she did her best to wait patiently and not to feel uneasy, though several times in the course of the next half-hour she went to the window to see

if there were no sign of the rain abating. Alas, no !
As heavily as ever, and even more steadily, it fell.
Something must be done she decided, and she was
just thinking of going to the kitchen to consult
Mrs. Crosby, when as she turned from the window
a curious object rolling or slowly hobbling down
the hill-side caught her view. That was the way
the children would come — what could that queer
thing be ? It was not too high, but far too broad
to be a child, and its way of moving was a sort of
jerky waddle through the bracken, very remarkable
to see. Whatever it was, dwarf or goblin, it found
its way difficult to steer, poor thing, for there, with
a sudden fly, over it went altogether and lay for a
moment or two struggling and twisting, till at last
it managed to get up again and painfully strove to
pursue its way.

The children's mother called their nurse.

" Esther," she said, " I cannot imagine what that
creature is coming down the road. But it is in
trouble evidently. Run off and see if you can
help." Off ran kind-hearted Esther, and soon she was
rewarded for her trouble. For as she got near to
the queer-shaped bundle, she saw two pairs of eyes
peering out at her, from the two arm - holes of

the waterproof cloak, and in a moment the mystery was explained. Ted, in his anxiety for the two girls, had wrapped them up *together* in the cloak which his mother had left, and literally "bundled" them off, with the advice to get home as quickly as possible, while he followed with his loaded truck, the wood covered as well as he could manage with leafy branches which he tore down.

But "possible" was not quickly at all in the case of poor Cissy and her companion. Polly was of a calm and placid nature, with something of the resignation to evils that one sees in the peasant class all over the world; but Narcissa, impulsive and sensitive, with her dainty dislike to mud, and her unaccustomedness to such adventures, could not long restrain her tears, and under the waterproof cloak she cried sadly, feeling frightened too at the angry gusts of rain and wind which sounded to her like the voices of ogres waiting to seize them and carry them off to some dreadful cavern.

The summit of their misfortunes seemed reached when they toppled over and lay for a moment or two helplessly struggling on the wet ground. But oh, what delight to hear Esther's kind voice, and how Cissy clung to her and sobbed out her woes!

o

She was more than half comforted again by the time they reached the farm-house, and just as mother was considering whether it would not be better to undress them in the kitchen before the fire and bring down their dry clothes, Master Ted, "very wet, yes very wet, oh very wet indeed," made his appearance, with rosy cheeks and a general look of self-satisfaction.

"Did they get home all right?" he said, cheerily. " It *was* a good thing you brought the cloak, mother. And the wood isn't so wet after all."

And an hour or two later, dried and consoled and sitting round the kitchen table for an extra good tea to which Mrs. Crosby had invited them, all the children agreed that after all the expedition had not turned out badly.

But the weather had changed there was no doubt; for the time at least the sunny days were over. The party in the farm-house had grown smaller too, for the uncles had had to leave, and even the children's father had been summoned away unexpectedly to London. And a day or two after the children's picnic their mother stood at the window rather anxiously looking out at the ever-falling rain.

" It really looks like as if it would *never* leave off,"

"Master Ted, very wet indeed, made his appearance with rosy cheeks and a general look of self-satisfaction."—P. 194.

she said, and there was some reason for her feeling
distressed. She had hoped for a letter from the
children's father that day, and very probably it was
lying at the two-miles-and-a-half-off post-office,
waiting for some one to fetch it. For it was not
one of the postman's days for coming round by the
farm-house; that only happened twice a week, but
hitherto this had been of little consequence to the
farm-house visitors. Their letters perhaps had not
been of such importance as to be watched for with
much anxiety, and in the fine weather it was quite
a pleasant little walk to the post-office by the fields
and the stepping-stones across the river. But all
this rain had so swollen the river that now the
stepping-stones were useless; there was nothing for
it but to take the long round by the road; and this
added to the difficulty in another way, for it was not
by any means every day that Mr. Crosby or his son
were going in that direction, or that they could, at
this busy season, spare a man so long off work. So
the children's mother could not see how she was to
get her letter if this rain continued—at least not for
several days, for the old postman had called yesterday—he would not take the round of the Skensdale
farm for other three or four days at least, and even

then, the post-office people were now so accustomed to some of the "gentry" calling for their letters themselves, that it was doubtful, not certain at least, if they would think of giving them to the regular carrier.　And with some anxiety, for her husband had gone to London on business of importance, Ted's mother went to bed.

Early next morning she was awakened by a tap at the door, a gentle little tap.　She almost fancied she had heard it before in her sleep without being really aroused.

"Come in," she said, and a very business-like figure, which at the first glance she hardly recognised, made its appearance.　It was Ted; dressed in waterproof from head to foot, cloak, leggings, and all, he really looked ready to defy the weather——a sort of miniature diver, for he had an oilskin cap on his head too, out of which gleamed his bright blue eyes, full of eagerness and excitement.

"Mother," he said, "I hope I haven't wakened you too soon.　I got up early on purpose to see about your letters.　It's still raining as hard as ever, and even if it left off, there'd be no crossing the stepping-stones for two or three days, Farmer Crosby says.　And he can't spare any one to-day to go to the post. I'm the only one that *can,* so I've got ready, and don't you think I'd better go at once?"

Ted's mother looked out of the window. Oh, how it was pouring! She thought of the long walk—the two miles and a half through the dripping grass of the meadows, along the muddy, dreary road, and all the way back again; and then the possibility of the swollen river having escaped its bounds where the road lay low, came into her mind and frightened her. For Ted was a little fellow still—only eleven and a half, and slight and delicate for his age. And then she looked at him and saw the eager readiness in his eyes, and remembered that he was quick-witted and careful, and she reflected also that he must learn, sooner or later, to face risks and difficulties for himself.

"Ted, my boy," she said, "it's very nice of you to have thought of it, and I know it would be a great disappointment if I didn't let you go. But you'll promise me to be very careful—to do nothing rash or unwise; if the river is over the road, for instance, or there is the least danger, you'll turn back?"

"Yes, mother, I'll be very careful, really," said Ted. "I'll do nothing silly. Good-bye, mother; thank you so much for letting me go. I've got my stick, but there's no use taking an umbrella."

And off he set; his mother watching him from the window as far as she could see him, trudging bravely along—a quaint little figure—through the pouring rain. For more than a mile she could see him making his way along the meadow path, gradually lessening as the distance increased, till a little black speck was all she could distinguish, and then it too disappeared round the corner.

And an hour or so later, there were warm, dry boots and stockings before the fire, which even in August the continued rain made necessary, and a "beautiful" breakfast of hot coffee, and a regular north-country rasher of bacon, and Mrs. Crosby's home-made bread and butter, all waiting on the table. And Ted's mother took up her post again to watch for the reappearance of the tiny black speck, which was gradually to grow into her boy. It did not tarry. As soon as was possible it came in sight.

"How quick he has been—my dear, clever, good little Ted!" his mother said to herself. And you may be sure that she, and Cissy too, were both at the door to meet the little human water-rat, dripping, dripping all over, like "Johnny Head-in-air" in old "Struwelpeter," but with eyes as bright as any water-rat's, and cheeks rosy with cold and exercise and pleasure all mixed together, who, before he said a word, held out the precious letter.

"Here it is, mother—from father, just as you expected. I do hope it's got good news."

How could it bring other? Mother felt before she opened it that it could not contain any but good news, nor did it. Then she just gave her brave little boy one good kiss and one hearty "Thank you, Ted." For she did not want to spoil him by over-praise, or to take the bloom off what he evidently thought nothing out of the common, by exaggerating it.

And Ted enjoyed his breakfast uncommonly, I can assure you. He was only eleven and a half. I think our Ted showed that he had a sweet and brave spirit of his own;—don't you, children?

CHAPTER XI.

"IT'S ONLY I, MOTHER."

" How well my own heart knew
That voice so clear and true."

THE summer in the wolds, so long looked forward
to, was over.　It had been very happy, in spite of
the rain having given the visitors at the Skensdale
farm-house rather more of his company than they
had bargained for, and it left many happy memories
behind it.

And the coming home again was happy too.
The days were beginning to "draw in" as people
say, and "home," with its coal-fires—which, though
not so picturesque, are ever so much *warmer* than
wood ones, I assure you—its well-closing doors and
shutters, its nice carpets and curtains, was after all
a better place for chilly days and evenings than
even the most interesting of farm-houses.　And Ted
had his school-work to think of too; he was anxious
to take a very good place at the next examinations,

for he was getting on for twelve, and "some day" he knew that he would have to go out into the world as it were, on his own account—to go away, that is to say, to a big boarding-school, as Percy had done before him.

He did work well, and he was rewarded, and this Christmas was a *very* happy one. There was plenty of skating, and Ted got on famously. Indeed, he learnt to be so clever at it, that Cissy used to feel quite proud, when people admired him for it, to think that he was her brother, though Ted himself took it quite simply. Skating was to him the greatest pleasure he knew. To feel oneself skimming along by one's own will, and yet with a power beyond oneself, was delightful past words.

"I do think," thought Ted to himself, one clear bright frosty day, when the sky was as blue, *almost*, as in summer, "I do think it's as nice as flying."

And then looking up, as he skimmed along, at the beautiful sky which winter or summer he loved so much, there came over him that same strange sweet *wonder*—the questioning he could not have put into words, as to whether the Heaven he often thought of in his dreamy childish way, was really up there, and what it was like, and what they did there.   It must be happy and bright—happier and brighter even than down here, because *there,* in some way that Ted knew that neither he nor the wisest of mankind could explain, one would be nearer God. But yet it was difficult to understand how it could be much brighter and happier than this happy life down below.   There was no good trying to understand, Ted decided.   *God* understood, and that was enough.   And as He had made us so happy here, He might be trusted to know what was best for us there.   Only—yes, that *was* the greatest puzzle of all, far more puzzling than anything else—*everybody* was not happy here—alas ! no, Ted knew enough to know that—many, many were not happy ; many, many were not good, and had never even had a chance of becoming so.   Ah, that *was* a puzzle !

"When I'm a man," thought Ted—and it was a thought that came to him often—"I'll try to do something for those poor boys in London."

For nothing had made more impression on Ted, during his stay in London, than the sight of the so-called "City Arabs," and all he had heard about them. He had even written a story on the subject, taking for his hero a certain "Tom," whose adventures and misadventures were most thrilling ; ending, for Ted

liked stories that ended well, with his happy adop-
tion into a kind-hearted family, such as it is to be
wished there were more of to be found in real life !
I should have liked to tell you this story, and some
day perhaps I shall do so, but not, I fear, in this
little book, for there are even a great many things
about Ted himself which I shall not have room for.

There were other pleasures besides skating this
Christmas time. Among these there was a very
delightful entertainment given by some of Ted's
father's and mother's friends to a very large party,
both old and young. It was a regular Christmas
gathering—so large that the great big old-fashioned
ball-room at the " Red Lion " was engaged for the
purpose.

Dear me, what a great many scenes this old ball-
room had witnessed ! Election contests without end,
during three-quarters of a century and more ; balls
of the old-world type, when the gentlemen had
powdered wigs and ribbon-tied " queues," which, no
doubt, you irreverent little people of the nineteenth
century would call " pig-tails ;" and my Lady Grizzle
from the hall once actually stuck in the doorway, so
ponderous was her head-gear, though by dint of good
management her hoop and furbelows had been got

through. And farther back still, in the Roundhead days, when—so ran the legend—a party of rollicking cavaliers, and a company commanded by one Captain Holdfast Armstrong, passed two succeeding nights in the Red Lion's ball-room, neither—so cleverly did the cautious landlord manage—having the least idea of the other's near neighbourhood.

But never had the old ball-room seen happier faces or heard merrier laughter than at this Christmas party; and among the happy faces none was brighter than our Ted's. He really did enjoy himself, though one of the youngest of the guests, for Cissy had been pronounced *too* young, but had reconciled herself to going to bed at her usual hour, by Ted's promise to tell her all about it the next day. And besides his boy friends—Percy, of course, who was home for the holidays, and Rex, and several others—Ted had another companion this evening whom he was very fond of. This was a little girl about his own age, named Gertrude, the daughter of a friend of his father's. I have not told you about her before, because, I suppose, I have had so many things to tell, that I have felt rather puzzled how to put them all in nicely, especially as they are all simple, every-day things, with nothing the least wonderful or re-

markable about them. Gertrude was a very dear
little girl; she almost seemed to Ted like another
kind of sister. He had Mabel, and Christine her
sister, as big ones, and Cissy as his own particular
little one, and Gertrude seemed to come in as a sort
of companion sister, between the big ones and the
little one. Ted was very rich in friends, you see,
friends of all kinds. He used often to count them
up and say so to himself.

Well, this evening of the big Christmas party
was, as I said, one of the happiest he had ever
known. All his friends were there—all looking as
happy as happy could be.

"When I'm a man," thought Ted to himself, "I'd
like to give parties like this every Christmas," and
as he looked round the room his eyes gleamed with
pleasure. Gertrude was standing beside him—they
were going to be partners in a country-dance, which
was a favourite of Ted's. Just then his mother
came up to where they were standing.

"Ted, my boy," she said, "I am going home now.
It is very late for you already—half-past twelve.
The others, however, are staying later, but I think
it is quite time for you and me to be going, don't
you?"

Ted's face clouded — a most unusual thing to happen.

"Gertrude isn't going yet," he said, "and Rex and his brothers; they're staying later. O mother, *must* I come now?"

His mother hesitated. She was always reluctant to disappoint the children if it could be helped, yet, on the other hand, she was even more anxious not to *spoil* them. But the sight of Ted's eager face carried the day.

"Ah well," she said, smiling, "I suppose I must be indulgent for once and go home without you. So good-night, Ted——you will come with the others—— I hope it won't be *very* late."

As she turned away, it struck her that Ted's face did not look *altogether* delighted.

"Poor Ted," she said to herself, "he doesn't like to see me go away alone." But hoping he would enjoy himself, and that he would not be *too* tired "to-morrow morning," she went home without any misgiving, and she was not sorry to go. She found the Christmas holidays and all they entailed more fatiguing than did the children, for whom all these pleasant things "grew" without preparation.

It was a rather dark night—so thought Ted's

mother to herself as she glanced out of her window
for a moment before drawing the curtains close and
going to bed—all the house was shut up, and all
those who had stayed at home fast asleep by this
time, and it had been arranged that the others should
let themselves in with a latch-key. Ted's mother
felt, therefore, rather surprised and a little startled
when she heard a bell ring; at first she could hardly
believe that she was not mistaken, and to be quite
sure she opened the window and called out " Is there
any one there ?" There was half a moment's silence,
then some one came out a little from under the porch,
where he had been standing since ringing the bell,
and a well-known voice replied—how clearly and
brightly its young tones rose up through the frosty
air—

"It is only I, mother. I thought I'd rather
come home after all."

"You, Ted," she replied ;—" you, and alone ?"

"Yes, mother. I thought somehow you'd like
better to have me, so I just ran home."

"And weren't you frightened, Ted ?" she said a
little anxiously, but with a glad feeling at her heart ;
"weren't you afraid to come through the lonely
streets, and the road, more lonely still, outside the

town ?   For it is very dark, and everything shut
up—weren't you afraid ?"

"Oh no, mother—not a bit," he replied, "only
just when I had left all the houses I did walk a
little faster, I think.   But I'm so glad I came, if
you're pleased, mother."

And when his mother had opened the door and
let him in and given him a good-night kiss even
more loving than usual, Ted went to bed and to
sleep with a light happy heart, and his mother, as
she too fell asleep, thanked God for her boy.

  *   *   *   *

I must now, I think, children, ask you to pass
over with me nearly a whole year of Ted's life.
These holidays ended, came, by slow degrees that
year, the always welcome spring; then sunny summer again, a bright and happy summer this, though
spent at my little friends' own home instead of at
the Skensdale farm-house; then autumn with its
shortening days and lengthening evenings, gradually
shortening and lengthening into winter again; till at
last Christmas itself, like the familiar figure of an
old friend, whom, just turning the corner of the road
where we live, we descry coming to visit us, was to
be seen not so far off.

Many things had happened during this year, which, though all such simple things, I should like to tell you of but for the old restrictions of time and space. And indeed I have to thank you for having listened to me so long, for I blame myself a little for not having told you more plainly at the beginning that it was *not* a regular "story" I had to tell you in the "carrots" coloured book this year, but just some parts, simple and real, of a child-life that I love to think of. And I would have liked to leave it here—for some reasons that is to say—or I would have liked to tell how Ted grew up into such a man as his boyhood promised—honest-hearted, loving, and unselfish, and as happy as a true Christmas child could not but be. But, dears, I *cannot* tell you this, for it was not to be so. Yet I am so anxious that the little book I have tried to write in such a way that his happy life and nature should be loved by other children—I am so anxious that the ending of this little book should not seem to you a *sad* one, at Christmas-time too of all times, that I find it a little difficult to say what has to be said. For in the truest sense the close of my book is *not* sad. I will just tell it simply as it really was, trusting that you will know I love you all too

P

well to wish to throw any cloud over your bright
faces and thoughts.

Well, as I said, this year had brought many little
events, some troubles of course, and much good, to
our Ted. He had grown a good deal taller, and
thinner too, and he never, even as a tiny toddler,
could have been called fat! But he was well and
strong, and had made good progress at school and
good progress too in other ways. He was getting
on famously at cricket and football, and was a first-
rate croquet-player, for croquet was then in fashion.
And the museum had not been neglected; it had
really grown into a very respectable and interesting
museum, so that not only Ted's own people and near
friends were pleased to see it, but even his parents'
friends, and sometimes others, again, who happened
to be visiting them, would ask the little collector to
admit them. I really think it would be a good
thing if more boys took to having museums; it
would be a good thing for them, for nothing can be
more amusing and interesting too, and a very good
thing for their friends, especially in bad weather or
in holiday-time, when now and then the hours hang
heavily on these young people's hands, and one is
inclined to wish that some fancy work for *boys* could

be invented. Ted's museum had grown very much, and was always a great resource for him and for Cissy too, for, to tell the truth, her tastes were *rather* boyish.

His library had grown too. I cannot tell you how many nice books he had, and still less could I tell you how he treasured them. When, through much service, some of them grew weak in the back, he would, though reluctantly, consent to have them re-bound ; and he had a pretty, and to my mind a touching, way of showing his affection for these old friends, which I never heard of in any other child. Before a book of his went to be bound he would carefully—tenderly I might almost say—cut off the old cover and lay it aside, and among the many sweet traces left by our boy—but I did not mean to say that, only as it came naturally of itself I will leave it—few went more to his mother's heart than to find in one of his drawers the packet carefully tied up of his dear books' old coats.

Nothing gave Ted so much pleasure as a present of a book. This Christmas he had set his heart on one, and Christmas was really coming so near that he had begun to think of presents, and to write out, as was his habit, a list of all the people in the house, putting opposite the name of each the present he had reason to think would be most acceptable. The list ended in a modest-looking "self," and opposite "self" was written "a book." But all the other presents would have to be thought over and consulted about with mother—all except hers of course, which in its turn would have to be discussed with his father or Mabel perhaps—ever so many times, before it came to the actual buying.

One Sunday—it was about three weeks to Christmas by this time—the head master of Ted's school, who was also a clergyman, mentioned after the usual service that he wished to have a special thanksgiving service this year for the good health that had been enjoyed by the boys this "half." It had been almost exceptionally good, he said; and he himself, for one, and he was sure every one connected with the school would feel the same, *was* very thankful for it.

Ted's mother and Mabel, who were both, as it happened, at the school chapel service that afternoon, glanced at their boy when this announcement was made. They knew well that, despite his merry heart, Ted was sensitive to things that do not affect all children, and they were not surprised to see his cheeks grow a little paler. There was something in the thought of this solemn Thanksgiving, in which he was to take part, that gave him a little of the same feeling as he had had long ago in the grand old church, when he looked up to the lofty roof, shrouded in a mystery of dim light his childish eyes could not pierce, and the sudden carillon broke out as if sung by the angels in heaven.

And a little chill struck to his mother's heart; she knew the service was a good and fitting acknowledgment of God's care, and yet a strange feeling went through her, for which she blamed herself, almost like that of the poor Irishwomen, who, when any one remarks on the beauty and healthiness of their children, hasten to cross themselves and to murmur softly "In a good hour be it spoken." For human nature, above all *mother* nature, is the same all the world over!

But on their way home she and Mabel talked it over, and decided that it was better to say nothing about it to Ted.

"It would only deepen the impression and *make* him nervous," said Mabel wisely.

A day or two later—a damp, rainy day it had been, there were a good many such about this time

—Ted's mother, entering the drawing-room in the evening, heard some one softly singing to himself, gently touching the piano at the same time. It was already dusk, and she went in very quietly. The little musician did not hear her, and she sat down in silence for a moment to listen, for it was Ted, and the song in his sweet, clear tones—tones with a strange touch of sadness in them like the church bells, was "Home, sweet home."

It brought the tears to her eyes.

"Ted," she said at last.

"O mother," he said, "I didn't know you were there."

"But you don't mind *me*," she said.

Ted hesitated.

"I don't know how it is, mother," he said, frankly. "It isn't as if I *could* sing, you know. But I can't even try to do it when anybody's there. Is it silly, mother?"

"It's very natural," she said, kindly. "But if it gives me pleasure to hear you?"

"Yes," he said, gently.

"And when you're a man I hope and think you may have a nice voice."

"Yes," he said again, rather absently.

Something in his tone struck his mother; it sounded *tired*.

"You're quite well, Ted, aren't you?" she said.

"Oh yes, mother—just a very little tired. It's been such a rainy day; it isn't like Christmas coming so soon, is it? There's no snow and no skating."

"No, dear."

"There was no snow the Christmas I was born, was there, mother?"

"No, dear," said his mother again.

Ted gave a little sigh.

"You're going to Rex's to-night; it is his party, isn't it?" she asked.

"Yes," he replied, "but I don't seem to care much to go."

"But you're quite well, I think," said his mother cheerfully. "It would be unkind not to go when they are all expecting you."

"Yes," said Ted. "It would be."

So he went off to get ready; and his mother felt pleased, thinking the dull weather had, for a wonder, affected his spirits, and that the merry evening with his friends would do him good.

CHAPTER XII.

THE WHITE CROSS.

" It is not growing like a tree
  In bulk, doth make man better be,
  Or standing long an oak, three hundred year.
  To fall a log at last, dry, bald, and sere.
          The lily of a day
          Is fairer far in May,
  Although it fade and die that night
  It was the plant and flower of light ;
  In small proportions we just beauties see,
  And in short measures life may perfect be."
          "Early Ripe."—BEN JONSON.

IT seemed as if she had been right. Ted came home with bright eyes and glowing cheeks, and said they had had an " awfully " merry evening. And his mother went to bed with an easy mind.

But the next morning she felt less happy again, for Ted was evidently not well. He was not very ill, but just not very well, and he hung about in an uninterested, unsettled way, quite unlike his usual busy briskness.

"He excites himself too much when he goes out, I think," said his father; "we really shall have to leave off ever letting him go out in the evening unless we are there ourselves;" and he looked a little anxiously at Ted as he spoke, though the boy had not heard what he said.

But again this slight anxiety passed by. Then came a change in the weather, and a sudden frost set in. Ted seemed to revive at once, and when he heard that there was to be a whole holiday for skating, no one was more eager about it than he. And, a little against her own feelings, his mother let him go.

"You must be careful, Ted," she said; "you are not yet looking as well as usual. And the ice cannot be very firm. Indeed, I almost doubt its bearing at all. A bath in icy water would not do you any good just now."

But Ted promised to be careful, and his mother knew she could trust him. Besides, several big boys were to be there, who would, she knew, look after him. So Ted went, and came home saying it had been as usual "awfully jolly;" but he did look tired, and owned himself rather so, even though well enough to go out again in the evening with the others, and to be one of the merriest at what the children called " a penny reading " together, at which each in turn of the little party of friends read or repeated or acted some story or piece of poetry for the amusement of the others.   And once again, but this was the last time she could do so, Ted's mother felt able to throw off the slight vague anxiety which had kept coming and going for the last few days about her little boy, and to go to sleep with an easy mind.

But the next morning, to his own and her disappointment, he woke " tired " again.   Only tired—he complained of nothing else, but he said he wished he need not go to school.   And that was *so* unlike Ted.

" Need I go, mother ?" he asked gently.

She looked at him doubtfully.

"It seems such a pity, dear—so near the examinations too.   And sometimes, you know, when you haven't felt quite well in the morning you have come back quite right again."

" Very well," said Ted, and he went off cheerfully enough.

But when he came back he was not all right as his mother had hoped ; the " tiredness" was greater, and he seemed to have caught cold, and the next morning, after a restless night, there was no longer any doubt that Ted was ill. Our dear little Ted— how quickly illness does its work—above all with children! Almost before one has realised its presence the rosy cheeks are pale and the bright eyes dimmed ; the sturdy legs grow weak and trembling, and the merry chatter ceases. Ah dear! what a sad, strange hush comes over a house where "one of the children" is ill.

The hush and the sadness came but gradually. Still, for a day or two, they hoped it was nothing very serious. On this first afternoon of Ted's really owning himself ill, two girl friends of Mabel's came, as had been arranged, to see the famous museum, usually such a pleasure to its owner to exhibit. But already how different all seemed!

"Mother, dear," he said, as if half reproaching himself for selfishness, "it sometimes almost seems a bother to have to show my museum;" but as it was considered better not to let him yield to the depression coming over him, he bravely roused himself and went through the little exhibition with his usual gentle courtesy. But this was the last effort of the kind possible for him.

Sunday and Monday found him weaker, and the

doctor's kind face grew graver. Still he was not *very* ill; only it began to seem as if he had not strength to resist what had not, at first, threatened seriously. And one day he made his mother's heart seem, for an instant, to stop beating, when, looking up wistfully, he said to her,

"Mother, I don't *think* I shall ever get better."

And the sad days and sadder nights went slowly on. Now and then there seemed a little sparkle of hope. Once Ted began to talk about meeting his dear Percy at the station, when he came home for the holidays, which made those about him hope he was feeling stronger; then, at another time, he said what a pity it would be not to be well by Christmas and by his birthday, and he smiled when his father told him, as was the case, that the doctor quite hoped he would be well by then; and one day when the post brought him his great wish—a beautiful book of travels—his face lighted up with pleasure, and, though not able to read it, the welcome present lay on his bed where he could see it and smile to himself to think it was there. There were happy times through his illness, weak and wearied though he grew, and now and then he seemed so bright that it was difficult, for a little, not to think him much better. But the illness which Ted had is a very deceitful one—it invisibly saps away the strength even when the worst sharp suffering is over—and slowly, slowly it came to be seen that his own feeling had been true; our Ted was not to get better.

One day a travelling merchant brought to the door a case of pretty Parian ornaments. White and pure they shone in the winter sunshine, and some one had the thought that "one of these might please Ted." So they were brought up for him to choose from. Poor Cissy! she would fain have carried them in; but alas! for fear of infection, she could not be allowed to see her brother, which made of these last days a double sorrow to her, though she did not know how ill he was. Ted touched the pretty things with his little thin hand.

"They are very pretty," he said. "I like this one best, please, mother."

"This one" was a snow-white cross, and his mother's heart ached with a strange thrill as she saw his choice; but she smiled as she placed it beside him, where it stood, ever in his sight, till his blue eyes could see it no more.

There came a morning on which the winter sun rose with a wonderful glory; gold and orange light seemed to fill the sky, as if in prelude to some splendid pageant. It was Sunday morning. Ted lay asleep, as if carved in marble, his little white face rested on the pillow, and as his mother turned from the marvellous beauty outside to the small figure that seemed to her, just then, the one thing in earth or sky, she whispered to herself what she felt to be the truth.

" It is his last Sunday with us. Before another my Ted will have· entered that city where there is no need of the sun, of which God Himself is the light. My happy Ted ! but oh, how shall we live without him ?"

She was right. Ted did not live to see Christmas or his birthday. Sweetly and peacefully, trusting God in death as he had trusted Him in life, the little fellow fearlessly entered the dark valley—the valley of the *shadow* of death only, for who can doubt that to such as Ted what *seems* death is but the entrance to fuller life ?

So, children, I will not say that this was the *end* of the simple life I have told you of—and in yet another way Ted lives—in the hearts of all that loved him his sweet memory can never die. And if I have been able to make any among you feel that you too love him, I cannot tell you how glad I shall be.

They laid him in a pretty corner of the little cemetery from which can be seen the old church Ted loved so well, and the beautiful chase, where he so often walked. And even in those midwinter days his little friend Gertrude found flowers for his grave. It was all she could do to show her love for him, she said, crying bitterly, for she might not see him to bid him good-bye, and her heart was very sore.

So it was with Christmas roses that the grave of our Christmas child was decked.

THE END.

Printed by R. & R. CLARK, *Edinburgh.*

MACMILLAN & CO.'S CATALOGUE of Works in BELLES LETTRES, *including Poetry, Fiction, etc.*

ADDISON, SELECTIONS FROM. By JOHN RICHARD GREEN, M.A., LL.D. (Golden Treasury Series.) 18mo. 4s. 6d.

ALLINGHAM. — LAWRENCE BLOOMFIELD IN IRELAND; or, THE NEW LANDLORD. By WILLIAM ALLINGHAM. New and Cheaper Issue, with a Preface. Fcap. 8vo, cloth. 4s. 6d.

THE BALLAD BOOK. Edited by WILLIAM ALLINGHAM. (Golden Treasury Series.) 18mo. 4s. 6d.

ALEXANDER, (C. F.) — THE SUNDAY BOOK OF POETRY FOR THE YOUNG. (Golden Treasury Series.) 18mo. 4s. 6d.

AN ANCIENT CITY, AND OTHER POEMS. — By A NATIVE OF SURREY. Extra fcap. 8vo. 6s.

ANDERSON. — BALLADS AND SONNETS. By ALEXANDER ANDERSON (Surfaceman). Extra fcap. 8vo. 5s.

ARCHER. — CHRISTINA NORTH. By E. M. ARCHER. New and Cheaper Edition. Crown 8vo. 6s.

UNDER THE LIMES. Second and Cheaper Edition. Crown 8vo. 6s.

ARNOLD. — THE POETICAL WORKS OF MATTHEW ARNOLD. Vol. I. EARLY POEMS, NARRATIVE POEMS, AND SONNETS. Vol. II. LYRIC, DRAMATIC, AND ELEGIAC POEMS. New and Complete Edition. Two Vols. Crown 8vo. Price 7s. 6d. each.

SELECTED POEMS OF MATTHEW ARNOLD. With Vignette engraved by C. H. JEENS (Golden Treasury Series.) 18mo. 4s. 6d. Large Paper Edition. Crown 8vo. 12s. 6d.

ART AT HOME SERIES. — Edited by W. J. LOFTIE, F.S.A.

A PLEA FOR ART IN THE HOUSE. With especial reference to the Economy of Collecting Works of Art, and the importance of Taste in Education and Morals. By W. J. LOFTIE, B.A., F.S.A. With Illustrations. Fifth Thousand. Crown 8vo. 2s. 6d.

SUGGESTIONS FOR HOUSE DECORATION IN PAINTING, WOOD-WORK, AND FURNITURE. By RHODA and AGNES GARRETT. With Illustrations. Sixth Thousand. Crown 8vo. 2s. 6d.

ART AT HOME SERIES—*continued*.

MUSIC IN THE HOUSE. By JOHN HULLAH. With Illustrations. Fourth Thousand. Crown 8vo. 2s. 6d.

THE DRAWING-ROOM; ITS DECORATIONS AND FURNITURE. By Mrs. ORRINSMITH. Illustrated. Fifth Thousand. Crown 8vo. 2s. 6d.

THE DINING-ROOM. By Mrs. LOFTIE. Illustrated. Fourth Thousand. Crown 8vo. 2s. 6d.

THE BED-ROOM AND BOUDOIR. By LADY BARKER. Illustrated. Fourth Thousand. Crown 8vo. 2s. 6d.

DRESS. By Mrs. OLIPHANT. Illustrated. Crown 8vo. 2s. 6d.

AMATEUR THEATRICALS. By WALTER H. POLLOCK and LADY POLLOCK. Illustrated by KATE GREENAWAY. Crown 8vo. 2s. 6d.

NEEDLEWORK. By ELIZABETH GLAISTER, Author of "Art Embroidery." Illustrated. Crown 8vo. 2s. 6d.

THE MINOR ARTS—PORCELAIN PAINTING, WOOD CARVING, STENCILLING, MODELLING, MOSAIC WORK, &c. By CHARLES G. LELAND. Illustrated. Crown 8vo. 2s 6d.

[Other Vols. in preparation.]

ATKINSON.—AN ART TOUR TO THE NORTHERN CAPITALS OF EUROPE. By J. BEAVINGTON ATKINSON. 8vo. 12s.

ATKINSON, (J. P.).—A WEEK AT THE LAKES, AND WHAT CAME OF IT; or, THE ADVENTURES OF MR. DOBBS AND HIS FRIEND MR. POTTS. A Series of Sketches by J. P. ATKINSON. Oblong 4to. 7s. 6d.

ATTWELL, HENRY. A BOOK OF GOLDEN THOUGHTS. (Golden Treasury Series.) 18mo. 4s. 6d.

BACON'S ESSAYS. Edited by W. ALDIS WRIGHT. (Golden Treasury Series.) 18mo. 4s. 6d.

BAKER.—CAST UP BY THE SEA; or, THE ADVENTURES OF NED GREY. By Sir SAMUEL BAKER, Pasha, F.R.G.S. With Illustrations by HUARD. Sixth Edition. Crown 8vo, cloth gilt. 6s.

BALLAD BOOK. — CHOICEST ANECDOTES AND SAYINGS. Edited by WILLIAM ALLINGHAM. (Golden Treasury Series.) 18mo. 4s. 6d.

BARKER (LADY).—A YEAR'S HOUSEKEEPING IN SOUTH AFRICA. With Illustrations. Cheaper Edition. Crown 8vo. 6s.

THE WHITE RAT and other Stories. Illustrated by W. J. HENNESSY. Globe 8vo. 4s 6d.

BEESLY.—STORIES FROM THE HISTORY OF ROME. By Mrs. BEESLY. Fcap. 8vo. 2s. 6d.

BETSY LEE ; A FO'C'S'LE YARN. Extra fcap. 8vo. 3s. 6d.

BLACK (W.).—Works by W. BLACK, Author of "A Daughter of Heth."

THE STRANGE ADVENTURES OF A PHAETON. Thirteenth Thousand. Illustrated. Crown 8vo. 6s.

A PRINCESS OF THULE. Fourteenth Thousand. Crown 8vo. 6s.

THE MAID OF KILLEENA, and other Stories. Fifth Thousand. Crown 8vo. 6s.

MADCAP VIOLET. Eighth Thousand. Crown 8vo. 6s.

GREEN PASTURES AND PICCADILLY. Cheaper Edition. Seventh Thousand. Crown 8vo. 6s.

MACLEOD OF DARE. With Illustrations. Cheaper Edition. Crown 8vo. 6s.

WHITE WINGS. A YACHTING ROMANCE. Three Vols. Crown 8vo. 31s. 6d.

BLACKIE.—THE WISE MEN OF GREECE. In a Series of Dramatic Dialogues. By J. S. BLACKIE, Professor of Greek in the University of Edinburgh. Crown 8vo. 9s.

GOETHE'S FAUST. Translated into English Verse, with Notes and Preliminary Remarks. By J. STUART BLACKIE, F.R.S.E. Crown 8vo. 9s.

BLAKISTON.—MODERN SOCIETY IN ITS RELIGIOUS AND SOCIAL ASPECTS. By PEYTON BLAKISTON, M.D., F.R S. Crown 8vo. 5s.

BORLAND HALL.—By the Author of " Olrig Grange." Crown 8vo. 7s.

BRAMSTON.—RALPH AND BRUNO. A Novel. By M. BRAMSTON. Two Vols. Crown 8vo. 21s.

BRIGHT.—A YEAR IN A LANCASHIRE GARDEN. By HENRY A. BRIGHT. Second Edition. Crown 8vo. 3s. 6d.

BROOKE.—THE FOOL OF QUALITY, or, THE HISTORY OF HENRY, EARL OF MORELAND. By HENRY BROOKE. Newly revised, with a Biographical Preface by the Rev. CHARLES KINGSLEY, M.A., Rector of Eversley. Crown 8vo. 6s.

BUNCE.—FAIRY TALES, THEIR ORIGIN AND MEANING. With some Account of the Dwellers in Fairy Land. By J. THACKRAY BUNCE. Extra fcap. 8vo. 3s. 6d.

BUNYAN'S PILGRIM'S PROGRESS. (Golden Treasury Series. 18mo. 4s. 6d.

BURNAND.—MY TIME, AND WHAT I'VE DONE WITH IT. By F. C. BURNAND. Crown 8vo. 6s.

a 2

BURNETT.—HAWORTH'S. A Novel. By FRANCES HODGSON BURNETT, Author of "That Lass o' Lowrie's." Crown 8vo. 6s.

LOUISIANA; and THAT LASS O' LOWRIE'S. Two Stories. Illustrated. Crown 8vo. 6s.

BURNS.—THE POETICAL WORKS OF. Edited from the best printed and manuscript Authorities, with Glossarial Index and a Biographical Memoir, by ALEXANDER SMITH. Two Vols. Fcap. 8vo, hand-made paper, with Portrait of Burns, and Vignette of the Twa Dogs, engraved by SHAW, and printed on India Paper. 12s.

COMPLETE WORKS OF. Edited with Memoir by ALEXANDER SMITH. (Globe Edition.) Globe 8vo. 3s. 6d.

CARROLL.—Works by "LEWIS CARROLL":—

ALICE'S ADVENTURES IN WONDERLAND. With Forty-two Illustrations by TENNIEL. 57th Thousand. Crown 8vo, cloth. 6s.

A GERMAN TRANSLATION OF THE SAME. With TENNIEL's Illustrations. Crown 8vo, gilt. 6s.

A FRENCH TRANSLATION OF THE SAME. With TENNIEL's Illustrations. Crown 8vo, gilt. 6s.

AN ITALIAN TRANSLATION OF THE SAME. By T. P. ROSSETTE. With TENNIEL's Illustrations. Crown 8vo. 6s.

THROUGH THE LOOKING-GLASS, AND WHAT ALICE FOUND THERE. With Fifty Illustrations by TENNIEL. Crown 8vo, gilt. 6s. 45th Thousand.

THE HUNTING OF THE SNARK. An Agony in Eight Fits. With Nine Illustrations by H. HOLIDAY. Crown 8vo, cloth extra, gilt edges. 4s. 6d. 18th Thousand.

DOUBLETS. A Word Puzzle. 18mo. 2s.

CAUTLEY.—A CENTURY OF EMBLEMS. By G. S. CAUTLEY, Vicar of Nettleden, Author of "The After Glow," etc. With numerous Illustrations by LADY MARION ALFORD, REAR-ADMIRAL LORD W. COMPTON, the Ven. LORD A. COMPTON, R. BARNES, J. D. COOPER, and the Author. Pott 4to, cloth elegant, gilt elegant. 10s. 6d.

CAVALIER AND HIS LADY. Selections from the Works of the First Duke and Duchess of Newcastle. With an Introductory Essay by E. JENKINS. (Golden Treasury Series.) 18mo. 4s. 6d.

CHRISTMAS CAROL (A.) Printed in Colours from Original Designs by Mr. and Mrs. TREVOR CRISPIN, with Illuminated Borders from MSS. of the 14th and 15th Centuries. Imp. 4to, cloth elegant. Cheaper Edition. 21s.

CHURCH (A. J.).—HORÆ TENNYSONIANÆ, Sive Eclogæ e Tennysono Latine redditæ. Cura A. J. CHURCH, A.M. Extra fcap. 8vo. 6s.

CLOUGH (ARTHUR HUGH).—THE POEMS AND PROSE REMAINS OF ARTHUR HUGH CLOUGH. With a Selection from his Letters, and a Memoir. Edited by his Wife. With Portrait. Two Vols. Crown 8vo. 21s.

THE POEMS OF ARTHUR HUGH CLOUGH, sometime Fellow of Oriel College, Oxford. Fifth Edition. Fcap. 8vo. 6s.

CLUNES.—THE STORY OF PAULINE: An Autobiography. By G. C. CLUNES. Crown 8vo. 6s.

COLERIDGE.—HUGH CRICHTON'S ROMANCE. A Novel. By CHRISTABEL R. COLERIDGE. Second Edition. Crown 8vo. 6s.

COLLECTS OF THE CHURCH OF ENGLAND. With a beautifully Coloured Floral Design to each Collect, and Illuminated Cover. Crown 8vo. 12s. Also kept in various styles of morocco.

COLQUHOUN.—RHYMES AND CHIMES. By F. S. COLQUHOUN (née F. S. FULLER MAITLAND). Extra fcap. 8vo. 2s. 6d.

COOPER.—SEBASTIAN. A Novel. By KATHERINE COOPER. Crown 8vo. 6s.

COWPER.—POETICAL WORKS. Edited, with Biographical Introduction, by Rev. W. BENHAM, B.D. (Globe Edition.) Globe 8vo. 3s. 6d.

DANTE; AN ESSAY. With a Translation of the "De Monarchia." By the Very Rev W. R. CHURCH, D.C.L., Dean of St. Paul's. Crown 8vo. 6s.

THE "DE MONARCHIA." Separately. 8vo. 4s. 6d.

THE PURGATORY. Edited, with Translation and Notes, by A. J. BUTLER. Post 8vo. 12s. 6d.

DAY.—BENGAL PEASANT LIFE. By the Rev. LAL BEHARI DAY. New Edition. Crown 8vo. 6s.

DAYS OF OLD; STORIES FROM OLD ENGLISH HISTORY. By the Author of "Ruth and Her Friends." New Edition. 18mo, cloth extra. 2s. 6d.

DEUTSCHE LYRIK. By Dr. BUCHHEIM. (Golden Treasury Series.) 18mo. 4s. 6d.

DILLWYN, (E. A.).—THE REBECCA RIOTER. A Story of Killay Life. Two Vols. Crown 8vo. 21s.

DOTTY, AND OTHER POEMS. By J. L. Extra fcap. 8vo. 3s. 6d.

DRYDEN.—POETICAL WORKS OF. Edited, with a Memoir, by W. D. CHRISTIE, M.A. (Globe Edition.) Globe 8vo. 3s. 6d.

DUFF (GRANT).—MISCELLANIES, POLITICAL and LITERARY. By the Right Hon. M. E. GRANT DUFF, M.P. 8vo. 10s. 6d.

DUNSMUIR (AMY).—VIDA; Study of a Girl. New Edition. Crown 8vo. 6s.

ELSIE; A LOWLAND SKETCH. By A. C. M. Crown 8vo. 6s.

ENGLISH MEN OF LETTERS. Edited by JOHN MORLEY. Crown 8vo. 2s. 6d.

JOHNSON. By LESLIE STEPHEN.

SCOTT. By R. H. HUTTON.

GIBBON. By J. C. MORISON.

SHELLEY. By J. A. SYMONDS.

HUME. By Professor HUXLEY.

GOLDSMITH. By WILLIAM BLACK.

DEFOE. By W. MINTO.

BURNS. By Principal SHAIRP.

SPENSER. By R. W. CHURCH.

THACKERAY. By ANTHONY TROLLOPE.

BURKE. By JOHN MORLEY.

MILTON. By MARK PATTISON.

HAWTHORNE. By HENRY JAMES, Junr.

SOUTHEY. By Professor DOWDEN.

CHAUCER. By A. W. WARD.

COWPER. By GOLDWIN SMITH.

BUNYAN. By J. A. FROUDE.

LOCKE. By T. FOWLER.

BYRON. By JOHN NICHOL.

ESTELLE RUSSELL. By the Author of " The Private Life of Galileo." New Edition. Crown 8vo. 6s.

EVANS.—Works by SEBASTIAN EVANS.

BROTHER FABIAN'S MANUSCRIPT, AND OTHER POEMS. Fcap. 8vo, cloth. 6s.

IN THE STUDIO: A DECADE OF POEMS. Extra fcap. 8vo. 5s.

FAIRY BOOK. By the Author of " John Halifax, Gentleman." (Golden Treasury Series.) 18mo. 4s. 6d.

FARRELL.—THE LECTURES OF A CERTAIN PROFESSOR. By the Rev. JOSEPH FARRELL. Crown 8vo. 7s. 6d.

FAWCETT.—TALES IN POLITICAL ECONOMY. By MILLICENT FAWCETT, Author of " Political Economy for Beginners." Globe 8vo. 3s.

FLEMING.—Works by GEORGE FLEMING.

A NILE NOVEL. Third and Cheaper Edition. Crown 8vo. 6s.

MIRAGE. A Novel. Cheaper Edition. Crown 8vo. 6s.

THE HEAD OF MEDUSA. A Novel. Three Volumes. Crown 8vo. 31s. 6d.

FLETCHER. — THOUGHTS FROM A GIRL'S LIFE. By LUCY FLETCHER. Second Edition. Fcap. 8vo. 4s. 6d.

FREEMAN.—HISTORICAL AND ARCHITECTURAL SKETCHES; CHIEFLY ITALIAN. By E. A. FREEMAN, D.C.L., LL.D. With Illustrations by the Author. Crown 8vo. 10s. 6d.

GARNETT. — IDYLLS AND EPIGRAMS. Chiefly from the Greek Anthology. By RICHARD GARNETT. Fcap. 8vo. 2s. 6d.

GILMORE.—STORM WARRIORS; or, LIFE-BOAT WORK ON THE GOODWIN SANDS. By the Rev. JOHN GILMORE, M.A., Rector of Holy Trinity, Ramsgate, Author of "The Ramsgate Life-Boat," in "Macmillan's Magazine." Second Edition. Crown 8vo. 6s.

GLOBE LIBRARY.—Globe 8vo. Cloth. 3s. 6d. each.

SHAKESPEARE'S COMPLETE WORKS. Edited by W. G. CLARK, M.A., and W. ALDIS WRIGHT, M.A., of Trinity College, Cambridge, Editors of the "Cambridge Shakespeare." With Glossary. pp. 1,075.

SPENSER'S COMPLETE WORKS. Edited from the Original Editions and Manuscripts, by R. MORRIS, with a Memoir by J. W. HALES. M.A. With Glossary. pp. lv., 736.

SIR WALTER SCOTT'S POETICAL WORKS. Edited with a Biographical and Critical Memoir by FRANCIS TURNER PALGRAVE, and copious Notes. pp. xliii., 559.

COMPLETE WORKS OF ROBERT BURNS.—THE POEMS. SONGS, AND LETTERS, edited from the best Printed and Manuscript Authorities. with Glossarial Index, Notes, and a Biographical Memoir by ALEXANDER SMITH. pp. lxii., 636.

ROBINSON CRUSOE. Edited after the Original Editions, with a Biographical Introduction by HENRY KINGSLEY. pp. xxxi., 607.

GOLDSMITH'S MISCELLANEOUS WORKS. Edited, with Biographical Introduction by Professor MASSON. pp. lx., 695.

POPE'S POETICAL WORKS. Edited, with Notes and Introductory Memoir, by ADOLPHUS WILLIAM WARD, M.A., Fellow of St. Peter's College, Cambridge, and Professor of History in Owens College, Manchester. pp. lii., 508.

DRYDEN'S POETICAL WORKS. Edited, with a Memoir, Revised Text, and Notes, by W. D. CHRISTIE, M.A., of Trinity College, Cambridge. pp. lxxxvi., 662.

COWPER'S POETICAL WORKS. Edited, with Notes and Biographical Introduction, by WILLIAM BENHAM. pp. lxxiii., 536.

MORTE D'ARTHUR.—SIR THOMAS MALORY'S BOOK OF KING, ARTHUR AND OF HIS NOBLE KNIGHTS OF THE ROUND TABLE. The original Edition of CAXTON, revised for Modern Use. With an Introduction by Sir EDWARD STRACHEY, Bart. pp. xxxvi., 509.

THE WORKS OF VIRGIL. Rendered into English Prose, with Introductions, Notes, Running Analysis, and an Index. By JAMES LONSDALE. M.A., late Fellow and Tutor of Balliol College, Oxford, and Classical Professor in King's College, London; and SAMUEL LEE, M.A., Latin Lecturer at University College, London. pp. 288.

GLOBE LIBRARY—*continued.*

THE WORKS OF HORACE. Rendered into English Prose with Introductions, Running Analysis, Notes and Index. By JOHN LONDSDALE, M.A., and SAMUEL LEE, M.A.

MILTON'S POETICAL WORKS, Edited, with Introductions, by Professor MASSON.

GOLDEN TREASURY SERIES.—Uniformly printed in 18mo., with Vignette Titles by J. E. MILLAIS, T. WOOLNER, W. HOLMAN HUNT, Sir NOEL PATON, ARTHUR HUGHES, &c. Engraved on Steel by JEENS, &c. Bound in extra cloth. 4s. 6d. each volume.

THE GOLDEN TREASURY OF THE BEST SONGS AND LYRICAL POEMS IN THE ENGLISH LANGUAGE. Selected and arranged, with Notes, by FRANCIS TURNER PALGRAVE.

THE CHILDREN'S GARLAND FROM THE BEST POETS. Selected and arranged by COVENTRY PATMORE.

THE BOOK OF PRAISE. From the best English Hymn Writers. Selected and arranged by LORD SELBORNE. *A New and Enlarged Edition.*

THE FAIRY BOOK; the Best Popular Fairy Stories. Selected and rendered anew by the Author of " John Halifax, Gentleman."

THE BALLAD BOOK. A Selection of the Choicest British Ballads. Edited by WILLIAM ALLINGHAM.

THE JEST BOOK. The Choicest Anecdotes and Sayings. Selected and arranged by MARK LEMON.

BACON'S ESSAYS AND COLOURS OF GOOD AND EVIL. With Notes and Glossarial Index. By W. ALDIS WRIGHT, M.A.

THE PILGRIM'S PROGRESS from this World to that which is to come. By JOHN BUNYAN.

THE SUNDAY BOOK OF POETRY FOR THE YOUNG. Selected and arranged by C. F. ALEXANDER.

A BOOK OF GOLDEN DEEDS of All Times and All Countries gathered and narrated anew. By the Author of " The Heir of Redclyffe."

THE ADVENTURES OF ROBINSON CRUSOE. Edited from the Original Edition by J. W. CLARK, M.A., Fellow of Trinity College, Cambridge.

THE REPUBLIC OF PLATO. Translated into English, with Notes, by J. Ll. DAVIES, M.A. and D. J. VAUGHAN, M.A.

THE SONG BOOK. Words and Tunes from the best Poets and Musicians. Selected and arranged by JOHN HULLAH, Professor of Vocal Music in King's College, London.

LA LYRE FRANCAISE. Selected and arranged, with Notes, by GUSTAVE MASSON, French Master in Harrow School.

TOM BROWN'S SCHOOLDAYS. By AN OLD BOY.

A BOOK OF WORTHIES. Gathered from the Old Histories and written anew by the Author of " The Heir of Redclyffe." With Vignette.

A BOOK OF GOLDEN THOUGHTS. By HENRY ATTWELL, Knight of the Order of the Oak Crown.

GOLDEN TREASURY SERIES—*continued.*

GUESSES AT TRUTH. By Two Brothers. New Edition.

THE CAVALIER AND HIS LADY. Selections from the Works of the First Duke and Duchess of Newcastle. With an Introductory Essay by Edward Jenkins, Author of "Ginx's Baby," &c.

THEOLOGIA GERMANICA. Which setteth forth many fair Lineaments of Divine Truth, and saith very lofty and lovely things touching a Perfect Life. Edited by Dr. Pfeiffer, from the only complete manuscript yet known. Translated from the German, by Susanna Winkworth. With a Preface by the Rev. Charles Kingsley, and a Letter to the Translator by the Chevalier Bunsen, D.D.

MILTON'S POETICAL WORKS. Edited, with Notes, &c., by Professor Masson. Two Vols. 18mo. 9*s.*

SCOTTISH SONG. A Selection of the Choicest Lyrics of Scotland. Compiled and arranged, with brief Notes, by Mary Carlyle Aitken.

DEUTSCHE LYRIK. The Golden Treasury of the best German Lyrical Poems, selected and arranged with Notes and Literary Introduction. By Dr. Buchheim.

ROBERT HERRICK.—SELECTIONS FROM THE LYRICAL POEMS OF. Arranged with Notes by F. T. Palgrave.

POEMS OF PLACES. Edited by H. W. Longfellow. England and Wales. Two Vols.

MATTHEW ARNOLD'S SELECTED POEMS. Also a Large Paper Edition. Crown 8vo. 12*s.* 6*d.*

THE STORY OF THE CHRISTIANS AND MOORS IN SPAIN. By Charlotte M. Yonge. With a Vignette by Holman Hunt.

LAMB'S TALES FROM SHAKESPEARE. Edited, with Preface, by the Rev. Alfred Ainger, Reader at the Temple.

WORDSWORTH'S SELECT POEMS. Chosen and Edited, with Preface, by Matthew Arnold. Also Large Paper Edition. Crown 8vo. 9*s.*

SHAKESPEARE'S SONGS AND SONNETS. Edited, with Notes, by Francis Turner Palgrave.

SELECTIONS FROM ADDISON. Edited by John Richard Green.

SELECTIONS FROM SHELLEY. Edited by Stopford A. Brooke. Also Large Paper Edition. Crown 8vo. 12*s.* 6*d.*

GOLDSMITH.—MISCELLANEOUS WORKS. Edited with Biographical Introduction, by Professor Masson. (Globe Edition) Globe 8vo. 3*s.* 6*d.*

GOETHE'S FAUST. Translated into English Verse, with Notes and Preliminary Remarks, by John Stuart Blackie, F.R.S.E., Professor of Greek in the University of Edinburgh. Crown 8vo. 9*s.*

GUESSES AT TRUTH. By Two Brothers. (Golden Treasury Series.) 18mo. 4*s.* 6*d.*

HAMERTON.—Works by P. G. HAMERTON.

ETCHING AND ETCHERS. Illustrated with Twelve new Etchings. Medium 8vo. Second Edition, revised.

A PAINTER'S CAMP IN THE HIGHLANDS. Second and Cheaper Edition. One Vol. Extra fcap. 8vo. 6s.

THE INTELLECTUAL LIFE. With Portrait of LEONARDO DA VINCI, etched by LEOPOLD FLAMENG. Second Edition. Crown 8vo. 10s. 6d.

THOUGHTS ABOUT ART. New Edition, Revised, with Notes and Introduction. Crown 8vo. 8s. 6d.

HARRY. A POEM. By the Author of "Mrs. Jerningham's Journal." Extra fcap. 8vo. 3s. 6d.

HAWTHORNE.—THE LAUGHING MILL; and Other Stories. By JULIAN HAWTHORNE. Cheaper Edition. Crown 8vo. 6s.

HEINE.—SELECTIONS FROM THE POETICAL WORKS OF HEINRICH HEINE. Translated into English. Crown 8vo. 4s. 6d.

HERRICK (ROBERT).—SELECTIONS FROM THE LYRICAL POEMS OF. Arranged with Notes by F. T. PALGRAVE. (Golden Treasury Series.) 18mo. 4s. 6d.

HIGGINSON.—MALBONE; An Oldport Romance. By T. W. HIGGINSON. Fcap. 8vo. 2s. 6d.

HILDA AMONG THE BROKEN GODS. By the Author of "Olrig Grange." Extra fcap. 8vo. 7s. 6d.

HOBDAY.—COTTAGE GARDENING; or, FLOWERS, FRUITS, AND VEGETABLES FOR SMALL GARDENS. By E. HOBDAY. Crown 8vo. 1s. 6d.

HOOPER AND PHILLIPS.—A MANUAL OF MARKS ON POTTERY AND PORCELAIN. A Dictionary of Easy Reference. By W. H. HOOPER and W. C. PHILLIPS. With numerous Illustrations. Second Edition, revised. 16mo. 4s. 6d.

HOPKINS.—ROSE TURQUAND. A Novel. By ELLICE HOPKINS. Cheaper Edition. Crown 8vo. 6s.

HORACE.—WORD FOR WORD FROM HORACE. The Odes literally versified. By W. T. THORNTON, C.B. Crown 8vo. 7s. 6d.

WORKS OF. Rendered into English Prose by JOHN LONSDALE, M.A. and SAMUEL LEE, M.A. (Globe Edition.) Globe 8vo. 3s. 6d.

HUNT.—TALKS ABOUT ART. By WILLIAM HUNT. With a Letter by J. E. MILLAIS. Crown 8vo. 3s. 6d.

IRVING.—Works by WASHINGTON IRVING.

OLD CHRISTMAS. From the Sketch Book. With upwards of 100 Illustrations by RANDOLPH CALDECOTT, engraved by J. D. COOPER. Second Edition. Crown 8vo. cloth elegant. *6s.*

BRACEBRIDGE HALL. With 120 Illustrations by R. CALDECOTT. Crown 8vo. cloth gilt. *6s.*

JAMES.—Works by HENRY JAMES, jun.

FRENCH POETS AND NOVELISTS. Crown 8vo. *8s. 6d.*

CONTENTS:—Alfred de Musset—Théophile Gautier—Baudelaire—Honoré le Balzac—George Sand—Turgénieff, etc.

THE EUROPEANS. A Novel. Cheaper Edition. Crown 8vo. *6s.*

THE AMERICAN. Crown 8vo. *6s.*

DAISY MILLER; and other Stories. Crown 8vo. *6s.*

RODERICK HUDSON. Crown 8vo. *6s.*

THE MADONNA OF THE FUTURE; and other Tales. Crown 8vo. *6s.*

JOUBERT.—PENSÉES OF JOUBERT. Selected and Translated with the Original French appended, by HENRY ATTWELL, Knight of the Order of the Oak Crown. Crown 8vo. *5s.*

KEARY (A.).—Works by ANNIE KEARY.

CASTLE DALY; THE STORY OF AN IRISH HOME THIRTY YEARS AGO. New Edition. Crown 8vo. *6s.*

JANET'S HOME. New Edition. Globe 8vo. *2s. 6d.*

CLEMENCY FRANKLYN. New Edition. Globe 8vo. *2s. 6d.*

OLDBURY. New and Cheaper Edition. Crown 8vo. *6s.*

A YORK AND A LANCASTER ROSE. Crown 8vo. *6s.*

A DOUBTING HEART. New Edition. Crown 8vo. *6s.*

THE HEROES OF ASGARD. Globe 8vo. *2s. 6d.*

KEARY (E.).—THE MAGIC VALLEY; or, PATIENT ANTOINE. With Illustrations by E. V. B. Globe 8vo. gilt. *4s. 6d.*

KINGSLEY.—Works by the Rev. CHARLES KINGSLEY, M.A., Rector of Eversley, and Canon of Westminster. Collected Edition. *6s. each.*

POEMS; including the Saint's Tragedy, Andromeda, Songs, Ballads, &c. Complete Collected Edition.

YEAST; a Problem.

ALTON LOCKE. New Edition. With a Prefatory Memoir by THOMAS HUGHES, Q.C., and Portrait of the Author.

HYPATIA; or, NEW FOES WITH AN OLD FACE.

GLAUCUS; or, THE WONDERS OF THE SEA-SHORE. With Coloured Illustrations.

KINGSLEY (C.)——*continued.*

WESTWARD HO! or, THE VOYAGES AND ADVENTURES OF SIR AMYAS LEIGH.

THE HEROES; or, GREEK FAIRY TALES FOR MY CHILDREN. With Illustrations.

TWO YEARS AGO.

THE WATER BABIES. A Fairy Tale for a Land Baby. With Illustrations by Sir NOEL PATON, R.S.A., and P. SKELTON.

THE ROMAN AND THE TEUTON. A Series of Lectures delivered before the University of Cambridge. With Preface by Professor MAX MÜLLER.

HEREWARD THE WAKE—LAST OF THE ENGLISH.

THE HERMITS.

MADAM HOW AND LADY WHY; or, FIRST LESSONS IN EARTH-LORE FOR CHILDREN.

AT LAST; A CHRISTMAS IN THE WEST INDIES. Illustrated.

PROSE IDYLLS. NEW AND OLD.

PLAYS AND PURITANS; and other HISTORICAL ESSAYS. With Portrait of Sir WALTER RALEIGH.

HISTORICAL LECTURES AND ESSAYS.

SANITARY AND SOCIAL LECTURES AND ESSAYS.

SCIENTIFIC LECTURES AND ESSAYS.

LITERARY AND GENERAL LECTURES.

HEALTH AND EDUCATION. New Edition. Crown 8vo. 6s.

PHAETHON; or, LOOSE THOUGHTS FOR LOOSE THINKERS. Crown 8vo. 2s.

TOWN GEOLOGY. Crown 8vo. 5s.

SELECTIONS FROM SOME OF THE WRITINGS OF THE REV. CHARLES KINGSLEY. Crown 8vo. 6s.

OUT OF THE DEEP. Words for the Sorrowful, from the writings of CHARLES KINGSLEY. Extra fcap. 8vo. 3s. 6d.

KINGSLEY (H.).—Works by HENRY KINGSLEY.

THE LOST CHILD. With Eight Illustrations by FRÖLICH. Crown 4to, cloth gilt. 3s. 6d.

TALES OF OLD TRAVEL. Re-narrated. With Eight full-page Illustrations by HUARD. Fifth Edition. Crown 8vo, cloth, extra gilt. 5s.

KNATCHBULL-HUGESSEN. —Works by E. H. KNATCHBULL-HUGESSEN, M.P.

CRACKERS FOR CHRISTMAS. More Stories. With Illustrations by JELLICOE and ELWES. Fifth Edition. Crown 8vo. 5s.

QUEER FOLK. FAIRY STORIES. Illustrated by S. E. WALLER. Fourth Edition. Crown 8vo, cloth gilt. 5s.

KNOX.—SONGS OF CONSOLATION. By ISA CRAIG KNOX. Extra fcap. 8vo, cloth extra, gilt edges. 4s. 6d.

LAMB'S TALES FROM SHAKESPEARE. Edited, with Preface, by the Rev. A. AINGER. (Golden Treasury Series.) 18mo. 4s. 6d.

LEADING CASES DONE INTO ENGLISH. By an Apprentice of Lincoln's Inn. Third Edition. Crown 8vo. 2s. 6d.

LELAND.—JOHNNYKIN AND THE GOBLINS. By C. G. LELAND, Author of "Hans Breitmann's Ballads." With numerous Illustrations by the Author. Crown 8vo. 6s.

LEMON (MARK).—THE JEST BOOK. (Golden Treasury Series.) 18mo. 4s. 6d.

LIFE AND TIMES OF CONRAD THE SQUIRREL. A Story for Children. By the Author of "Wandering Willie," "Effie's Friends," &c. With a Frontispiece by R. FARREN. Second Edition. Crown 8vo. 3s. 6d.

LITTLE ESTELLA, and other FAIRY TALES FOR THE YOUNG. 18mo, cloth extra. 2s. 6d.

LOFTIE.—FORTY-SIX SOCIAL TWITTERS. By Mrs. LOFTIE. Second Edition. 16mo. 2s. 6d.

LORNE.—Works by the MARQUIS OF LORNE :—

GUIDO AND LITA: A TALE OF THE RIVIERA. A Poem. Third Edition. Small 4to, cloth elegant. With Illustrations. 7s. 6d.

THE BOOK OF THE PSALMS, LITERALLY RENDERED IN VERSE. With Three Illustrations. Third Edition. Crown 8vo. 7s. 6d.

LOWELL.—COMPLETE POETICAL WORKS of JAMES RUSSELL LOWELL. With Portrait, engraved by JEENS. 18mo, cloth extra. 4s. 6d.

LYTTELTON.—Works by LORD LYTTELTON.

THE "COMUS" OF MILTON, rendered into Greek Verse. Extra fcap. 8vo. 5s.

THE "SAMSON AGONISTES" OF MILTON, rendered into Greek Verse. Extra fcap. 8vo. 6s. 6d.

MACLAREN.—THE FAIRY FAMILY. A Series of Ballads and Metrical Tales illustrating the Fairy Mythology of Europe. By ARCHIBALD MACLAREN. With Frontispiece, Illustrated Title, and Vignette. Crown 8vo, gilt. 5s.

MACMILLAN'S MAGAZINE.—Published Monthly. Price 1s. Vols. I. to XLII. are now ready. 7s. 6d. each.

MACMILLAN'S POPULAR NOVELS.— In Crown 8vo, cloth. Price 6s. each Volume :—

By William Black.

A PRINCESS OF THULE.

MADCAP VIOLET.

THE MAID OF KILLEENA; and other Tales.

THE STRANGE ADVENTURES OF A PHAETON. Illustrated.

GREEN PASTURES AND PICCADILLY.

MACLEOD OF DARE. Illustrated.

MACMILLAN'S POPULAR NOVELS—*continued.*

By Charles Kingsley.

TWO YEARS AGO.
"WESTWARD HO!"
ALTON LOCKE. With Portrait.

HYPATIA.
YEAST.
HEREWARD THE WAKE.

By the Author of "John Halifax, Gentleman."

THE HEAD OF THE FAMILY. Illustrated.
THE OGILVIES. Illustrated.

AGATHA'S HUSBAND. Illustrated.
OLIVE. Illustrated.

By Charlotte M. Yonge.

THE HEIR OF REDCLYFFE. With Illustrations.
HEARTSEASE. With Illustrations.
THE DAISY CHAIN. With Illustrations.
THE TRIAL: More Links in the Daisy Chain. With Illustrations.
HOPES AND FEARS. Illustrated.
DYNEVOR TERRACE. With Illustrations.
MY YOUNG ALCIDES. Illustrated.
THE PILLARS OF THE HOUSE. Two Vols. Illustrated.

CLEVER WOMAN OF THE FAMILY. Illustrated.
THE YOUNG STEPMOTHER. Illustrated.
THE DOVE IN THE EAGLE'S NEST. Illustrated.
THE CAGED LION. Illustrated.
THE CHAPLET OF PEARLS. Illustrated.
LADY HESTER, and THE DANVERS PAPERS. Illustrated.
THE THREE BRIDES. Two Vols. Illustrated.

By Frances H. Burnett.

HAWORTH'S.
"LOUISIANA" and "THAT LASS O' LOWRIE'S." Two Stories. Illustrated.

By Lady Augusta Noel.

OWEN GWYNNE'S GREAT WORK.

FROM GENERATION TO GENERATION.

By Mrs. Oliphant.

YOUNG MUSGRAVE.
THE CURATE IN CHARGE.

A SON OF THE SOIL.

By Annie Keary.

CASTLE DALY.

OLDBURY.

A YORK AND A LANCASTER ROSE.
A DOUBTING HEART.

By George Fleming.

A NILE NOVEL.

MIRAGE.

MACMILLAN'S POPULAR NOVELS—*continued.*

By Henry James, Junr.

THE EUROPEANS.

THE AMERICAN.

DAISY MILLER, AN INTERNA-
TIONAL EPISODE, FOUR
MEETINGS.

THE MADONNA OF THE
FUTURE, and other Tales.

RODERICK HUDSON.

TOM BROWN'S SCHOOLDAYS.

TOM BROWN AT OXFORD.

THE FOOL OF QUALITY. By
H. BROOKE.

REALMAH. By the Author of
" Friends in Council."

PATTY. By Mrs. MACQUOID.

THE BERKSHIRE LADY. By
Mrs. MACQUOID.

HUGH CRICHTON'S ROMANCE.
By C. R. COLERIDGE.

MY TIME, AND WHAT I'VE
DONE WITH IT. By F. C.
BURNAND.

ROSE TURQUAND. By ELLICE
HOPKINS.

OLD SIR DOUGLAS. By the
Hon. Mrs. NORTON.

SEBASTIAN. By KATHARINE
COOPER.

THE LAUGHING MILL; and
other Tales. By JULIAN HAW-
THORNE.

THE HARBOUR BAR.

CHRISTINA NORTH. By E. M.
ARCHER.

UNDER THE LIMES. By E. M.
ARCHER.

BENGAL PEASANT LIFE. By
LAL BEHARI DAY.

VIRGIN SOIL. By TOURGENIEF.

VIDA. The Study of a Girl. By
AMY DUNSMUIR.

MACQUOID.—Works by KATHARINE S. MACQUOID.

PATTY. Third and Cheaper Edition. Crown 8vo. 6s.

THE BERKSHIRE LADY. Crown 8vo. 6s.

MAGUIRE.—YOUNG PRINCE MARIGOLD, AND OTHER FAIRY
STORIES. By the late JOHN FRANCIS MAGUIRE, M.P. Illustrated by S. E.
WALLER. Globe 8vo, gilt. 4s. 6d.

MAHAFFY.—Works by J. P. MAHAFFY, M.A., Fellow of Trinity College,
Dublin:—

SOCIAL LIFE IN GREECE FROM HOMER TO MENANDER. Third
Edition, enlarged, with New Chapter on Greek Art. Crown 8vo. 9s.

RAMBLES AND STUDIES IN GREECE. Illustrated. Second Edition,
revised and enlarged, with Map. Crown 8vo. 10s. 6d.

MASSEY.—SONGS OF THE NOONTIDE REST. By LUCY MASSEY,
Author of " Thoughts from a Girl's Life." Fcap. 8vo, cloth extra. 4s. 6d.

MASSON (GUSTAVE)—LA LYRE FRANCAISE. Selected and
arranged with Notes. (Golden Treasury Series.) 18mo. 4s. 6d.

MASSON (Mrs.).—THREE CENTURIES OF ENGLISH POETRY:
being selections from Chaucer to Herrick, with Introductions and Notes by Mrs.
MASSON and a general Introduction by Professor MASSON. Extra fcap. 8vo.
3s. 6d.

MASSON (Professor):—Works by DAVID MASSON, M.A., Professor of Rhetoric and English Literature in the University of Edinburgh.

WORDSWORTH, SHELLEY, KEATS, AND OTHER ESSAYS. Crown 8vo. 5s.

CHATTERTON: A Story of the Year 1770. Crown 8vo. 5s.

THE THREE DEVILS: LUTHER'S, MILTON'S AND GOETHE'S; and other Essays. Crown 8vo. 5s.

MAZINI.—IN THE GOLDEN SHELL: A Story of Palermo. By LINDA MAZINI. With Illustrations. Globe 8vo, cloth gilt. 4s. 6d.

MERIVALE.—KEATS' HYPERION, rendered into Latin Verse. By C. MERIVALE, B.D. Second Edition. Extra fcap. 8vo. 3s. 6d.

MILNER.—THE LILY OF LUMLEY. By EDITH MILNER. Crown 8vo. 7s. 6d.

MILTON'S POETICAL WORKS. Edited with Text collated from the best Authorities, with Introduction and Notes, by DAVID MASSON. Three Vols. 8vo. 42s. With three Portraits engraved by C. H. JEENS. (Uniform with the Cambridge Shakespeare.) (Golden Treasury Edition.) By the same Editor. With Two Portraits. Two Vols. 18mo. 9s. (Globe Edition.) By the same Editor. Globe 8vo. 3s. 6d.

MISTRAL (F.).—MIRELLE, a Pastoral Epic of Provence. Translated by H. CRICHTON. Extra fcap. 8vo. 6s.

MITFORD (A. B.).—TALES OF OLD JAPAN. By A. B. MITFORD, Second Secretary to the British Legation in Japan. With Illustrations drawn and cut on Wood by Japanese Artists. New and Cheaper Edition. Crown 8vo. 6s.

MOLESWORTH.—Works by Mrs. MOLESWORTH (ENNIS GRAHAM).

GRANDMOTHER DEAR. Illustrated by WALTER CRANE. Eighth Thousand. Extra fcap. 8vo, cloth gilt. 4s. 6d.

TELL ME A STORY. Illustrated by WALTER CRANE. Globe 8vo, gilt. 4s. 6d. Fifth Thousand.

"CARROTS"; JUST A LITTLE BOY. Illustrated by WALTER CRANE. Ninth Thousand. Globe 8vo, gilt. 4s. 6d.

THE CUCKOO CLOCK. Illustrated by WALTER CRANE. Eighth Thousand. Globe 8vo, gilt. 4s. 6d.

THE TAPESTRY ROOM. Illustrated by WALTER CRANE. Globe 8vo, gilt. 4s. 6d.

A CHRISTMAS CHILD. Illustrated by WALTER CRANE. Globe 8vo. 4s. 6d.

MORTE D'ARTHUR.—SIR THOMAS MALORY'S BOOK OF KING ARTHUR AND OF HIS NOBLE KNIGHTS OF THE ROUND TABLE. (Globe Edition.) Globe 8vo. 3s. 6d.

MOULTON.—SWALLOW FLIGHTS. Poems by LOUISA CHANDLER MOULTON. Extra fcap. 8vo. 4s. 6d.

MOULTRIE.—POEMS by JOHN MOULTRIE. Complete Edition. Two Vols. Crown 8vo. 7s. each.

> Vol. I. MY BROTHER'S GRAVE, DREAM OF LIFE, &c. With Memoir by the Rev. Prebendary COLERIDGE.
> Vol. II. LAYS OF THE ENGLISH CHURCH, and other Poems. With notices of the Rectors of Rugby, by M. H. BLOXHAM, F.R.A.S.

MRS. JERNINGHAM'S JOURNAL. A Poem purporting to be the Journal of a Newly-married Lady. Third Edition. Fcap. 8vo. 3s. 6d.

MUDIE.—STRAY LEAVES. By C. E. MUDIE. New Edition. Extra fcap. 8vo. 3s. 6d. Contents :—"His and Mine"—"Night and Day"—"One of Many," &c.

MURRAY.—ROUND ABOUT FRANCE. By E. C. GRENVILLE MURRAY. Crown 8vo. 7s. 6d.

MYERS (ERNEST).—Works by ERNEST MYERS.

THE PURITANS. Extra fcap. 8vo, cloth. 2s. 6d.

POEMS. Extra fcap. 8vo. 4s. 6d.

MYERS (F. W. H.).—POEMS. By F. W. H. MYERS. Containing "St. Paul," "St. John," and others. Extra fcap. 8vo. 4s. 6d.

ST. PAUL. A Poem. New Edition. Extra fcap. 8vo. 2s. 6d.

NICHOL.—HANNIBAL, A HISTORICAL DRAMA. By JOHN NICHOL, B.A., Oxon., Regius Professor of English Language and Literature in the University of Glasgow. Extra fcap. 8vo. 7s. 6d.

NINE YEARS OLD.—By the Author of "St. Olave's," "When I was a Little Girl," &c. Illustrated by FRÖLICH. Fourth Edition. Extra fcap. 8vo, cloth gilt. 4s. 6d.

NOEL.—BEATRICE AND OTHER POEMS. By the HON. RODEN NOEL. Fcap. 8vo. 6s.

NOEL (LADY AUGUSTA).—Works by LADY AUGUSTA NOEL.

OWEN GWYNNE'S GREAT WORK. Cheaper Edition. Crown 8vo. 6s.

FROM GENERATION TO GENERATION. Crown 8vo. 6s.

NORTON.—Works by the Hon. Mrs. NORTON.

THE LADY OF LA GARAYE. With Vignette and Frontispiece. Eighth Edition. Fcap. 8vo. 4s. 6d.

OLD SIR DOUGLAS. New Edition. Crown 8vo. 6s.

OLIPHANT.—Works by Mrs. OLIPHANT.

AGNES HOPETOUN'S SCHOOLS AND HOLIDAYS. New Edition, with Illustrations. Globe 8vo. 2s. 6d.

A SON OF THE SOIL. New Edition. Crown 8vo. 6s.

THE CURATE IN CHARGE. Sixth Edition. Crown 8vo. 6s.

b

OLIPHANT—*continued*.

THE MAKERS OF FLORENCE : Dante, Giotto, Savonarola, and their City. With Illustrations from Drawings by Professor Delamotte, and a Steel Portrait of Savonarola, engraved by C. H. JEENS. Second Edition with Preface. Medium 8vo. Cloth extra. 21*s*.

YOUNG MUSGRAVE. Cheaper Edition. Crown 8vo. 6*s*.

THE BELEAGUERED CITY. Crown 8vo. 10*s*. 6*d*.

HE THAT WILL NOT WHEN HE MAY. Three Vols. Crown 8vo. 31*s*. 6*d*.

DRESS. Illustrated. Crown 8vo. 2*s*. 6*d*.   [*Art at Home Series*.

OUR YEAR. A Child's Book, in Prose and Verse. By the Author of "John Halifax, Gentleman." Illustrated by CLARENCE DOBELL. Royal 16mo. 3*s*. 6*d*.

PAGE:—THE LADY RESIDENT, by HAMILTON PAGE. Three Vols. ⎡Crown 8vo. 31*s*. 6*d*.

PALGRAVE.—Works by FRANCIS TURNER PALGRAVE, M.A., late Fellow of Exeter College, Oxford.

THE FIVE DAYS' ENTERTAINMENTS AT WENTWORTH GRANGE. A Book for Children. With Illustrations by ARTHUR HUGHES, and Engraved Title-Page by JEENS. Small 4to, cloth extra. 6*s*.

LYRICAL POEMS. Extra fcap. 8vo. 6*s*.

ORIGINAL HYMNS. Third Edition, enlarged 18mo. 1*s*. 6*d*.

GOLDEN TREASURY OF THE BEST SONGS AND LYRICS. Edited by F. T. PALGRAVE. 18mo. 4*s*. 6*d*.

SHAKESPEARE'S SONNETS AND SONGS. Edited by F. T. PALGRAVE. With Vignette Title by JEENS. (Golden Treasury Series.) 18mo. 4*s*. 6*d*.

THE CHILDREN'S TREASURY OF LYRICAL POETRY. Selected and arranged with Notes by F. T. PALGRAVE. 18mo. 2*s*. 6*d*. And in Two Parts, 1*s*. each.

HERRICK: SELECTIONS FROM THE LYRICAL POEMS. With Notes. (Golden Treasury Series.) 18mo. 4*s*. 6*d*.

PATER.—THE RENAISSANCE. Studies in Art and Poetry. By WALTER PATER, Fellow of Brasenose College, Oxford. Second Edition, Revised, with Vignette engraved by C. H. JEENS. Crown 8vo. 10*s*. 6*d*.

PATMORE.—THE CHILDREN'S GARLAND, from the Best Poets. Selected and arranged by COVENTRY PATMORE. New Edition. With Illustrations by J. LAWSON. Crown 8vo, gilt. 6*s*. (Golden Treasury Edition.) 18mo. 4*s*. 6*d*.

PEEL.—ECHOES FROM HOREB, AND OTHER POEMS. By EDMUND PEEL, Author of "An Ancient City," &c. Crown 8vo. 3*s*. 6*d*.

PEMBER.—THE TRAGEDY OF LESBOS. A Dramatic Poem. By E. H. PEMBER. Fcap. 8vo. 4*s*. 6*d*.

PHILLIPS (S. K.).—ON THE SEABOARD; and Other Poems. By SUSAN K. PHILLIPS. Second Edition. Crown 8vo. 5*s*.

PHILPOT.—A POCKET OF PEBBLES, WITH A FEW SHELLS; Being Fragments of Reflection, now and then with Cadence, made up mostly by the Sea-shore. By the Rev. W. B. PHILPOT. Second Edition, picked, sorted, and polished anew; with Two Illustrations by GEORGE SMITH. Fcap. 8vo. 5s.

PLATO.—THE REPUBLIC OF. Translated into English with Notes by J. LL DAVIES, M.A., and D. J. VAUGHAN, M.A. (Golden Treasury Series.) 18mo. 4s. 6d.

POEMS OF PLACES—(ENGLAND AND WALES). Edited by H. W. LONGFELLOW. (Golden Treasury Series.) 18mo. 4s. 6d.

POETS (ENGLISH).—SELECTIONS, with Critical Introductions by various writers, and a general Introduction by MATTHEW ARNOLD. Edited by T. H. WARD, M.A. Four Vols. Crown 8vo. 7s. 6d. each.

Vol. I. CHAUCER TO DONNE.

Vol. II. BEN JONSON TO DRYDEN.

Vols. III. and IV. in the Press.

POOLE.—PICTURES OF COTTAGE LIFE IN THE WEST OF ENGLAND. By MARGARET E. POOLE. New and Cheaper Edition. With Frontispiece by R. FARREN. Crown 8vo. 3s. 6d.

POPE.—POETICAL WORKS OF. Edited with Notes and Introductory Memoir by ADOLPHUS WILLIAM WARD, M.A. (Globe Edition.) Globe 8vo. 3s. 6d.

POPULATION OF AN OLD PEAR TREE. From the French of E. VAN BRUYSSEL. Edited by the Author of "The Heir of Redclyffe." With Illustrations by BECKER. Cheaper Edition. Crown 8vo, gilt. 4s. 6d.

POTTER.—LANCASHIRE MEMORIES. By LOUISA POTTER. Crown 8vo. 6s.

PRINCE FLORESTAN OF MONACO, THE FALL OF. By HIMSELF. New Edition, with Illustration and Map. 8vo, cloth extra, gilt edges. 5s. A French Translation. 5s. Also an Edition for the People. Crown 8vo. 1s.

QUIN.—GARDEN RECEIPTS. Edited by CHARLES QUIN. Crown 8vo. 2s. 6d.

RACHEL OLLIVER.—A Novel. Three Vols. Crown 8vo. 31s. 6d.

REALMAH.—By the Author of "Friends in Council. Crown 8vo. 6s.

RHOADES.—POEMS. By JAMES RHOADES. Fcap. 8vo. 4s. 6d.

RICHARDSON.—THE ILIAD OF THE EAST. A Selection of Legends drawn from Valmiki's Sanskrit Poem, "The Ramayana." By FREDERIKA RICHARDSON. Crown 8vo. 7s. 6d.

ROBINSON.—GEORGE LINTON; or, THE FIRST YEARS OF AN ENGLISH COLONY. By JOHN ROBINSON, F.R.G.S. Crown 8vo. 7s. 6d.

b 2

ROBINSON CRUSOE. Edited with Biographical Introduction by HENRY KINGSLEY. (Globe Edition.) Globe 8vo. 3s. 6d.—Golden Treasury Edition. Edited by J. W. CLARK, M.A. 18mo. 4s. 6d.

ROSSETTI.—Works by CHRISTINA ROSSETTI.

POEMS. Complete Edition. containing "Goblin Market," "The Prince's Progress," &c. With Four Illustrations. Extra fcap. 8vo. 6s.

SPEAKING LIKENESSES. Illustrated by ARTHUR HUGHES. Crown 8vo, gilt edges. 4s. 6d.

RUTH AND HER FRIENDS. A Story for Girls. With a Frontispiece. Seventh Edition. Globe 8vo. 2s. 6d.

SCOURING OF THE WHITE HORSE; OR, THE LONG VACATION RAMBLE OF A LONDON CLERK. Illustrated by DOYLE. Imp. 16mo. Cheaper Issue. 3s. 6d.

SCOTT (SIR WALTER.).—POETICAL WORKS OF. Edited with a Biographical and Critical Memoir by FRANCIS TURNER PALGRAVE. (Globe Edition.) Globe 8vo. 3s. 6d.

SCOTTISH SONG.—A SELECTION OF THE CHOICEST LYRICS OF SCOTLAND. By MARY CARLYLE AITKEN. (Golden Treasury Series.) 18mo. 4s. 6d.

SELBORNE (LORD).—THE BOOK OF PRAISE. From the best English Hymn writers. (Golden Treasury Series.) 18mo. 4s. 6d.

SHAKESPEARE.—The Works of WILLIAM SHAKESPEARE. Cambridge Edition. Edited by W. GEORGE CLARK, M.A., and W. ALDIS WRIGHT, M.A. Nine Vols. 8vo, cloth.

SHAKESPEARE'S COMPLETE WORKS. Edited, by W. G. CLARK, M.A., and W. ALDIS WRIGHT, M.A. (Globe Edition.) Globe 8vo. 3s. 6d.

SHAKESPEARE'S SONGS AND SONNETS. Edited, with Notes, by FRANCIS TURNER PALGRAVE. (Golden Treasury Series) 18mo. 4s. 6d.

SHAKESPEARE'S PLAYS. An attempt to determine the Chronological Order. By the Rev. H. PAINE STOKES, B.A. Extra fcap. 8vo. 4s. 6d.

SHAKESPEARE'S TEMPEST. Edited, with Glossarial and Explanatory Notes, by the Rev. J. M. JEPHSON. New Edition. 18mo. 1s.

SHELLEY.—POEMS OF. Edited by STOPFORD A. BROOKE. (Golden Treasury Series.) 18mo. 4s. 6d. Also a fine Edition printed on hand-made paper. Crown 8vo. 12s. 6d.

SLIP (A) IN THE FENS.—Illustrated by the Author. Crown 8vo. 6s.

SMEDLEY.—TWO DRAMATIC POEMS. By MENELLA BUTE SMEDLEY. Author of "Lady Grace," &c. Extra fcap. 8vo. 6s.

SMITH.—POEMS. By CATHERINE BARNARD SMITH. Fcap. 8vo. 5s.

SMITH (REV. WALTER).—HYMNS OF CHRIST AND THE CHRISTIAN LIFE. By the Rev. WALTER C. SMITH, M.A. Fcap. 8vo. 6s.

SONG BOOK. WORDS AND TUNES FROM THE BEST POETS AND MUSICIANS. Selected and arranged by JOHN HULLAH. (Golden Treasury Series.) 18mo. 4s. 6d.

SPENSER.—COMPLETE WORKS OF. Edited by the Rev. R. MORRIS, M.A., LL.D., with a Memoir by J. W. HALES, M.A. (Globe Edition.) Globe 8vo. 3s. 6d.

STEPHEN (C. E.).—THE SERVICE OF THE POOR; being an Inquiry into the Reasons for and against the Establishment of Religious Sisterhoods for Charitable Purposes. By CAROLINE EMILIA STEPHEN. Crown 8vo. 6s. 6d.

STEPHENS (J. B.).—CONVICT ONCE. A Poem. By J. BRUNTON STEPHENS. Extra fcap. 8vo. 3s. 6d.

STREETS AND LANES OF A CITY: Being the Reminiscences of AMY DUTTON. With a Preface by the BISHOP OF SALISBURY. Second and Cheaper Edition. Globe 8vo. 2s. 6d.

THOMPSON.—A HANDBOOK TO THE PUBLIC PICTURE GALLERIES OF EUROPE. With a brief sketch of the History of the various Schools of Painting from the thirteenth century to the eighteenth, inclusive. By KATE THOMPSON. Third Edition, Revised and Enlarged. With numerous Illustrations. Crown 8vo. 7s. 6d.

THEOLOGIA GERMANICA. Translated from the German by SUSANNA WINKWORTH. (Golden Treasury Series.) 18mo. 4s. 6d.

TOM BROWN'S SCHOOL DAYS. By AN OLD BOY. With Seven Illustrations by A. HUGHES and SYDNEY HALL. Crown 8vo. 6s.; Golden Treasury Edition. 4s. 6d.; People's Edition. 2s.

TOM BROWN AT OXFORD. New Edition. With Illustrations. Crown 8vo. 6s.

TOURGENIEF.—VIRGIN SOIL. By I. TOURGENIEF. Translated by ASHTON W. DILKE. Cheaper Edition. Crown 8vo. 6s.

TRENCH.—Works by R. CHENEVIX TRENCH, D.D., Archbishop of Dublin. (For other Works by this Author, see THEOLOGICAL, HISTORICAL, and PHILOSOPHICAL CATALOGUES.)

POEMS. Collected and arranged anew. Fcap. 8vo. 7s. 6d.

HOUSEHOLD BOOK OF ENGLISH POETRY. Selected and arranged, with Notes, by Archbishop TRENCH. Third Edition, revised. Extra fcap. 8vo. 5s. 6d.

SACRED LATIN POETRY, Chiefly Lyrical. Selected and arranged for Use. By Archbishop TRENCH. Third Edition, Corrected and Improved. Fcap. 8vo. 7s.

TURNER.—Works by the Rev. CHARLES TENNYSON TURNER.

SONNETS. Dedicated to his Brother, the Poet Laureate. Fcap. 8vo. *4s. 6d.*
SMALL TABLEAUX. Fcap. 8vo. *4s. 6d.*

TYRWHITT.—OUR SKETCHING CLUB. Letters and Studies on Land-scape Art. By the Rev. R. ST. JOHN TYRWHITT. M.A. With an Authorised Reproduction of the Lessons and Woodcuts in Professor Ruskin's "Elements of Drawing." Second Edition. Crown 8vo. *7s. 6d.*

UNDER THE LIMES. By the Author of "Christina North." Second Edition. Crown 8vo. *6s.*

VIRGIL.—THE WORKS OF. Rendered into English Prose. By JOHN LONSDALE, M.A., and SAMUEL LEE, M.A. (Globe Edition.) Globe 8vo. *3s. 6d.*

WEBSTER.—Works by AUGUSTA WEBSTER.

DRAMATIC STUDIES. Extra fcap. 8vo. *5s.*

A WOMAN SOLD, AND OTHER POEMS. Crown 8vo. *7s. 6d*

PORTRAITS. Second Edition. Extra fcap. 8vo. *3s. 6d.*

MEDEA OF EURIPIDES. Literally translated into English Verse. Extra fcap. 8vo. *3s. 6d.*

THE AUSPICIOUS DAY. A Dramatic Poem. Extra fcap. 8vo. *5s.*

YU-PE-YA'S LUTE. A Chinese Tale in English Verse. Extra fcap. 8vo. *3s. 6d.*

A HOUSEWIFE'S OPINIONS. Crown 8vo. *7s. 6d.*

WHEN I WAS A LITTLE GIRL. By the Author of "St. Olaves." Illustrated by L. FRÖLICH. Globe 8vo. *2s. 6d.*

WHITE.—RHYMES BY WALTER WHITE. 8vo. *7s 6d.*

WHITTIER.—JOHN GREENLEAF WHITTIER'S POETICAL WORKS. Complete Edition, with Portrait engraved by C. H. JEENS. 18mo. *4s. 6d.*

WILLOUGHBY.—FAIRY GUARDIANS. A Book for the Young. By F. WILLOUGHBY. Illustrated. Crown 8vo, gilt. *5s.*

WOLF.—THE LIFE AND HABITS OF WILD ANIMALS. Twenty Illustrations by JOSEPH WOLF, engraved by J. W. and E. WHYMPER. With descriptive Letter-press by D. G. ELLIOT, F.L.S. Super royal 4to, cloth extra, gilt edges. *21s.*

Also. an Edition in royal folio, Proofs before Letters, each Proof signed by the Engravers.

WOOLNER.—MY BEAUTIFUL LADY. By THOMAS WOOLNER. With a Vignette by A. HUGHES. Third Edition. Fcap. 8vo. *5s.*

WORDS FROM THE POETS. Selected by the Editor of "Rays of Sunlight." With a Vignette and Frontispiece. 18mo, limp. *1s.*

WORDSWORTH.—SELECT POEMS OF. Chosen and Edited, with Preface, by MATTHEW ARNOLD. (Golden Treasury Series.) 18mo. 4s. 6d. Fine Edition. Crown 8vo, hand-made paper, with Portrait of Wordsworth, engraved by C. H. JEENS, and Printed on India Paper. 9s.

YONGE (C. M.).—New Illustrated Edition of Novels and Tales by CHARLOTTE M. YONGE.

In Sixteen Monthly Volumes :—

Vol. I. THE HEIR OF REDCLYFFE. With Illustrations by KATE GREENAWAY. Crown 8vo. 6s.

II. HEARTSEASE. With Illustrations by KATE GREENAWAY. Crown 8vo. 6s.

III. HOPES AND FEARS. With Illustrations by HERBERT GANDY. Crown 8vo. 6s.

IV. DYNEVOR TERRACE. With Illustrations by ADRIAN STOKES.

V. THE DAISY CHAIN. Illustrated by J. P. ATKINSON.

VI. THE TRIAL. Illustrated by J. P. ATKINSON.

VII. & VIII. THE PILLARS OF THE HOUSE; or, UNDER WODE, UNDER RODE. Illustrated by HERBERT GANDY. Two Vols. Crown 8vo. 6s. each.

IX. THE YOUNG STEPMOTHER. New Edition. Illustrated by MARIAN HUXLEY. Crown 8vo. 6s.

X. CLEVER WOMAN OF THE FAMILY. New Edition. Illustrated by ADRIAN STOKES. Crown 8vo. 6s.

XI. THE THREE BRIDES. Illustrated by ADRIAN STOKES. Crown 8vo. 6s.

XII. MY YOUNG ALCIDES; or, A FADED PHOTOGRAPH. Illustrated by ADRIAN STOKES. Crown 8vo. 6s.

XIII. THE CAGED LION. Illustrated by W. J. HENNESSY. Crown 8vo. 6s.

XIV. THE DOVE IN THE EAGLE'S NEST. Illustrated by W. J. HENNESSY. Crown 8vo. 6s.

XV. THE CHAPLET OF PEARLS; or, THE WHITE AND BLACK RIBAUMONT. Illustrated by W. J. HENNESSY. Crown 8vo. 6s.

XVI. LADY HESTER AND THE DANVERS PAPERS. Illustrated by JANE E. COOK. Crown 8vo. 6s.

YONGE (C.M.).—

THE PRINCE AND THE PAGE. A Tale of the Last Crusade. Illustrated New Edition. 18mo. 2s. 6d.

THE LANCES OF LYNWOOD. New Edition. With Coloured Illustrations. 18mo. 4s. 6d.

THE LITTLE DUKE: RICHARD THE FEARLESS. New Edition Illustrated. 18mo. 2s. 6d.

A BOOK OF GOLDEN DEEDS OF ALL TIMES AND ALL COUNTRIES. Gathered and Narrated Anew. (Golden Treasury Series.) 4s. 6d. Cheap Edition. 1s.

A BOOK OF WORTHIES. (Golden Treasury Series.) 18mo. 4s. 6d.

YONGE (C. M.)—*continued.*

THE STORY OF THE CHRISTIANS AND MOORS IN SPAIN. (Golden Treasury Series.) 18mo. 4s. 6d.

CAMEOS FROM ENGLISH HISTORY. From Rollo to Edward II. Extra fcap. 8vo. 5s. Third Edition, enlarged. 5s.

Second Series. THE WARS IN FRANCE. Third Edition. Extra fcap. 8vo. 5s.

Third Series. THE WARS OF THE ROSES. Extra fcap. 8vo. 5s.

Fourth Series. REFORMATION TIMES. Extra fcap. 8vo. 5s.

P's AND Q's; or. THE QUESTION OF PUTTING UPON. With Illustrations by C. O. Murray. New Edition. Globe 8vo, cloth gilt. 4s. 6d.

MAGNUM BONUM; or, MOTHER CAREY'S BROOD. Three Vols. Crown 8vo. 31s. 6d.

BYEWORDS: A COLLECTION OF TALES NEW AND OLD. Crown 8vo. 6s.

LOVE AND LIFE. Two Vols. Crown 8vo. 12s.

www.ingramcontent.com/pod-product-compliance
Lightning Source LLC
Chambersburg PA
CBHW020348030726
47496CB00007B/2048